CONTENTS

William Sydney Porter (September 11, 1862 – June 5, 1910), known by his pen name **O. Henry**, was an American short story writer. His stories are known for their surprise endings.

Early life:

William Sidney Porter was born on September 11, 1862, in Greensboro, North Carolina. He changed the spelling of his middle name to Sydney in 1898. His parents were Dr. Algernon Sidney Porter (1825–88), a physician, and Mary Jane Virginia Swaim Porter (1833–65). William's parents had married on April 20, 1858. When William was three, his mother died from tuberculosis, and he and his father moved into the home of his paternal grandmother. As a child, Porter was always reading, everything from classics to dime novels; his favorite works were

Lane's translation of One Thousand and One Nights and Burton's Anatomy of Melancholy.

Porter graduated from his aunt Evelina Maria Porter's elementary school in 1876. He then enrolled at the Lindsey Street High School. His aunt continued to tutor him until he was fifteen. In 1879, he started working in his uncle's drugstore and in 1881, at the age of nineteen, he was licensed as a pharmacist. At the drugstore, he also showed off his natural artistic talents by sketching the townsfolk.

Cabbages and Kings is a 1904 novel written by O. Henry, set in a fictitious Central American country called the Republic of Anchuria. It takes its title from the poem "The Walrus and the Carpenter", featured in Lewis Carroll's Through the Looking Glass. Its plot contains famous elements in the poem: shoes and ships and sealing wax, cabbages and kings.The novel contains various short stories, all of which occur in Anchuria, and are connected to each other.

CABBAGES AND KINGS

"The time has come," the Walrus said,
" To talk of many things ; Of shoes and ships and sealing-wax,
And cabbages and kings."
THE WALRUS AND THE CARPENTER
CABBAGES AND KINGS
THE PROEM:
By the Carpenter

THEY will tell you in Anchuria, that President Miraflores, of that volatile republic, died by his own hand in the coast town of Coralio; that he had reached thus far in flight from the inconveniences of an imminent revolution; and that one hundred thou sand dollars, government funds, which he carried with him in an American leather valise as a souvenir of his tempestuous administration, was never after ward recovered.

For a real, a boy will show you his grave. It is back of the town near a little bridge that spans a mangrove swan: p. A plain slab of wood stands at its head. Soi ic one has burned upon the headstone with a hot ire n this inscription:

RAMON ANGEL DE LAS CRUZES

Y MIRAFLORES PRESIDENTE DE LA REPUBLICA

DE ANCHURIA QUE SEA SU JUEZ DIOS

It is characteristic of this buoyant people that they pursue no man beyond the grave. " Let God be his judge!" — Even with the hundred thousand unfound, though greatly coveted, the hue and cry went no fur ther than that.

To the stranger or the guest the people of Coralio will relate the story of the tragic end of their former president; how he strove to escape from the country with the public funds and also with Dona Isabel Guilbert, the young American opera singer; and how, being apprehended by members of the opposing polit ical party in Coralio, he shot himself through the head rather than give up the funds, and, in conse quence, the Senorita Guilbert. They will relate further that Dona Isabel, her adventurous bark of fortune shoaled by the simultaneous loss of her dis tinguished admirer and the souvenL* hundred thou sand, dropped anchor on this stagnar/ coast, await ing a rising tide.

They say, in Coralio, that she found a prompt and prosperous tide in the form of Frank Goodwin, an American resident of the town, an investor who had grown wealthy by dealing in the products of the coun try — a banana king, a rubber prince, a sarsaparilla, indigo, and mahogany baron. The Senorita Guil-bert, you will be told, married Senor Goodwin one month after the president's death, thus, in the very moment when Fortune had ceased to smile, wresting from her a gift greater than the prize withdrawn.

Of the American, Don Frank Goodwin, and of his wife the natives have nothing but good to say. Don Frank has lived among them for years, and has com pelled their respect. His lady is easily queen of what social life the sober coast affords. The wife of the governor of the district, herself, who was of the proud Castilian family of Monteleon y Dolorosa de los Santos y Mendez, feels honoured to unfold her nap kin with olive-hued, ringed hands at the table of Senora Goodwin. Were you to refer (with your northern prejudices) to the vivacious past of Mrs. Goodwin when her audacious and gleeful abandon in light opera captured the mature president's fancy,

or to her share in that statesman's downfall and mal feasance, the Latin shrug of the shoulder would be your only answer and rebuttal. What prejudices there were in Coralio concerning Senora Goodwin seemed now to be in her favour, whatever they had been in the past.

It would seem that the story is ended, instead of begun; that the close of a tragedy and the climax of a romance have covered the ground of interest; but, to the more curious reader it shall be some slight in struction to trace the close threads that underlie the> ingenuous web of circumstances.

The headpiece bearing the name of President Miraflores is daily scrubbed with soap-bark and sand. An old half-breed Indian tends the grave with fidelity and the dawdling minuteness of inherited sloth. He chops down the weeds and ever-springing grass with his machete, he plucks ants and scorpions and beetles from it with his horny fingers, and sprinkles its turf with water from the plaza fountain. There is no grave anywhere so well kept and ordered.

Only by following out the underlying threads will it be made clear why the old Indian, Galvez, is

secretly paid to keep green the grave of President Miraflores by one who never saw that unfortunate statesman in life or in death, and why that one was wont to walk in the twilight, casting from a distance looks of gentle sadness upon that unhonoured mound.

Elsewhere than at Coralio one learns of the im petuous career of Isabel Guilbert. New Orleans gave her birth and the mingled French and Spanish Creole nature that tinctured her life with such tur bulence and warmth. She had little education, but a knowledge of men and motives that seemed to have come by instinct. Far beyond the common woman was she endowed with intrepid rashness, with a love for the pursuit of adventure to the brink of danger, and with desire for the pleasures of life. Her spirit was one to chafe under any curb; she was Eve after the fall, but before the bitterness of it was felt. She wore life as a rose in her bosom.

Of the legion of men who had been at her feet it was said that but one was so fortunate as to engage her fancy. To President Miraflores, the brilliant but unstable ruler of Anchuria, she yielded the key to her resolute heart. How, then, do we find her (as

the Coralians would have told you) the wife of Frank Goodwin, and happily living a life of dull and dreamy inaction ?

The underlying threads reach far, stretching across the sea. Following them out it will be made plain why "Shorty" O'Day, of the Columbia Detective Agency, resigned his position. And, for a lighter pastime, it sh,all be a duty and a pleasing sport to wander with Momus beneath the tropic stars where Melpomene once stalked austere. Now to cause laughter to echo from those lavish jungles and frowning crags where formerly rang the cries of pirates' victims; to lay aside pike and cutlass and attack with quip and jollity; to draw one saving titter of mirth from the rusty casque of Romance—this were pleasant to do in the shade of the lemon-trees on that coast that is curved like lips set for smiling.

For there are yet tales of the Spanish Main. That segment of continent washed by the tempestuous Ca ribbean, and presenting to the sea a formidable border of tropical jungle topped by the overweening Cordil leras, is still begirt by mystery and romance. In past times buccaneers and revolutionists roused the echoes

of its cliffs, aud the condor wheeled perpetually above where, in the green groves, they made food for him with their matchlocks and toledos. Taken and re taken by sea rovers, by adverse powers and by sudden uprising of rebellious factions, the historic 300 miles of adventurous coast has scarcely known for hun dreds of years whom rightly to call its master. Pi-zarro, Balboa, Sir Francis Drake, and Bolivar did what they couJd to make it a part of Christendom. Sir John Morgan> Lafitte and other eminent swash bucklers bombarded and pounded it in the name of Abaddon.

The game still goes on. The guns of the rovers are silenced; bul th*e tintype man, the enlarged photo graph brigand, tho kodaking tourist and the scouts of the gentle brigade of fakirs have found it out, and carry on the work The hucksters of Germany, France, and Sicily new bag its small change across their counters. Gentlemen adventurers throng the waiting-rooms of its rulers wi A proposals for railways and concessions. The little opfra-bouffe nations play at government and intrigue until some day a big:, silent gunboat glides into the offing and Wires then, not to

break their toys. And with these changes comes also the small adventurer, with empty pockets to fill, light of heart, busy-brained — the modern fairy prince, bearing an alarm clock with which, more surely than by the sentimental kiss, to awaken the beautiful tropics from their centuries' sleep. Gene rally he wears a shamrock, which he matches pride-fully against the extravagant palms; and it is he who has driven Melpomene to the wings, and set Comedy to dancing before the footlights of the South ern Cross.

So, there is a little tale to tell of many things. Per haps to the promiscuous ear of the Walrus it shall come with most avail; for in it there are indeed shoes and ships and sealing-wax and cabbage-palms and presidents instead of kings.

Add to these a little love and counterplotting, and scatter everywhere throughout the maze a trail of tropical dollars — dollars warmed no more by the torrid sun than by the hot palms of the scouts of For tune — and, after all, here seems to be Life, itself, with talk enough to weary the most garrulous of Walruses.

CHAPTER ONE

" Fox-in-the-Morning "
VORALIO reclined, in the mid-day heat, like some vacuous beauty lounging in a guarded harem. The town lay at the sea's edge on a strip of alluvial coast. It was set like a little pearl in an emerald band. Be hind it, and seeming almost to topple, imminent, above it, rose the sea-following range of the Cordil leras. In front the sea was spread, a smiling jailer, but even more incorruptible than the frowning moun tains. The waves swished along the smooth beach; the parrots screamed in the orange and ceiba-trees; the palms waved their limber fronds foolishly like an awkward chorus at the prima donna's cue to enter. Suddenly the town was full of

excitement. A native boy dashed down a grass-grown street, shriek*

ing: " Busca el SeHor Goodwin. Ha venido un

teUgrajo por el!"

The word passed quickly. Telegrams do not often come to anyone in Coralio. The cry for Senor Good win was taken up by a dozen officious voices. The main street running parallel to the beach became pop ulated with those who desired to expedite the delivery of the despatch. Knots of women with complexions varying from palest olive to deepest brown gath ered at street corners and plaintively carolled: " Un telfyrafo por Senor Goodwin!" The comandante, Don Senor el Coronel Encarnaci6n Rios, who was loyal to the Ins and suspected Goodwin's devotion to the Outs, hissed: " Aha! " and wrote in his secret memorandum book the accusive fact that Senor Goodwin had on that momentous date received a telegram.

In the midst of the hullabaloo a man stepped to the door of a small wooden building and looked out. Above the door was a sign that read "Keogh and Clancy"— a nomenclature that seemed not to be in digenous to that tropical soil. The man in the door was Billy Keogh, scout of fortune and progress and

latter-day rover of the Spanish Main. Tintypes and photographs were the weapons with which Keogh and Clancy were at that time assailing the helpless shores. Outside the shop were set two large frames filled with specimens of their art and skill.

Keogh leaned in the doorway, his bold and humor ous countenance wearing a look of interest at the unusual influx of life and sound into the street. When the meaning of the disturbance became clear to him he placed a hand beside his mouth and shouted: " Hey! Frank!" in such a robustious voice that the feeble clamour of the natives was drowned and silenced.

Fifty yards away, on the seaward side of the street, stood the abode of the consul for the United States. Out from the door of this building tumbled Goodwin at the call. He had been smoking with Willard Ged-die, the consul, on the back porch of the consulate, which was conceded to be the coolest spot in Coralio.

" Hurry up," shouted Keogh. " There's a riot in town on account of a telegram that's come for you. You want to be careful about these things, my boy. It won't do to trifle with the feelings of the public

this way. You'll be getting a pink note some day with violet scent on it; and then the country'll be steeped in the throes of a revolution."

Goodwin had strolled up the street and met the boy with the message. The ox-eyed women gazed at him with shy admiration, for his type drew them. He was big, blonde, and jauntily dressed in white linen, with buckskin zapatos. His manner was courtly, with a sort of kindly truculence in it, tem pered by a merciful eye. When the telegram had been delivered, and the bearer of it dismissed with a gratuity, the relieved populace returned to the con tiguities of shade from which curiosity had drawn it — the women to their baking in the mud ovens under the orange-trees, or to the interminable comb ing of their long, straight hair; the men to their cigarettes and gossip in the cantinas.

Goodwin sat on Keogh's doorstep, and read his telegram. It was from Bob Englehart, an American, who lived in San Mateo, the capital city of Anchuria, eighty miles in the interior. Englehart was a gold miner, an ardent revolutionist and "good people." That he was a man of resource and imagination was

proven by the telegram he had sent. It had been his task to send a confidential message to his friend in Coralio. This could not have been accomplished in either Spanish or English, for the eye politic in An-churia was an active one. The Ins and the Outs were perpetually on their guard.

But Englehart was a diplomatist. There existed but one code upon which he might make requisition with promise of safety — the great and potent code of Slang. So, here is the message that slipped, unconstrued, through the fingers of curious officials, and came to the eye of Goodwin:

"His Nibs skedaddled yesterday per jack-rabbit line with all the coin in the kitty and the bundle of muslin he's spoony about. The boodle is six figures short. Our crowd in good shape, but we need the spondulicks. You collar it. The main guy and the dry goods are headed for the briny. You know what to do. BOB."

This screed, remarkable as it was, had no mystery for Goodwin. He was the most successful of the small advance-guard of speculative Americans that had invaded Anchuria, and he had not reached that enviable pinnacle without having well exercised the arts of foresight and deduction. Ho ft.ad taken up political intrigue as a matter of business. He was acute enough to wield a certain influence among the leading schemers, and he was prosperous enough to be able to purchase the respect of the petty office holders. There was always a revolutionary party; and to it he had always allied himself; for the adhe rents of a new administration received the rewards of their labours. There was now a Liberal party seeking to overturn President Miraflores. If the wheel successfully revolved, Goodwin stood to win a concession to 30,000 manzanas of the finest coffee lands in the interior. Certain incidents in the recent career of President Miraflores had excited a shrewd suspicion in Goodwin's mind that the government was near a dissolution from another cause than that of a revolution, and now Englehart's telegram had come as a corroboration of his wisdom.

The telegram, which had remained unintelligible to the Anchurian linguists who had applied to it in vain their knowledge of Spanish and elemental English, conveyed a stimulating piece of news to Goodwin's understanding. It informed him that the president of the republic had decamped from the capital city with the contents of the treasury. Furthermore, that he was accompanied in his flight by that winning adventuress Isabel Guilbert, the opera singer, whose troupe of performers had been entertained by the president at San Mateo during the past month on a scale less modest than that with which royal visitors are often content. The reference to the "jack-rab bit line " could mean nothing else than the mule-back system of transport that prevailed between Coralio and the capital. The hint that the "boodle" was " six figures short" made the condition of the national treasury lamentably clear. Also it was convincingly true that the ingoing party — its way now made a pacific one — would need the " spondulicks." Un less its pledges should be fulfilled, and the spoils held for the delectation of the victors, precarious indeed, would be the position of the new government. There fore it was exceeding necessary to "collar the main guy," and recapture the sinews of war and govern ment.

Goodwin handed the message to Keogh.

"Read that, Billy," he said. "It's from Bob Englehart. Can you manage the cipher?"

Keogh sat in the other half of the doorway, and carefully perused the telegram.

" 'Tis not a cipher," he said, finally. " 'Tis what they call literature, and that's a system of language put in the mouths of people that they've never been introduced to by writers of imagination. The maga zines invented it, but I never knew before that Presi dent Norvin Green had stamped it with the seal of his approval. 'Tis now no longer literature, but lan guage. The dictionaries tried, but they couldn't make it go for anything but dialect. Sure, now that the Western Union indorses it, it won't be long till a race of people will spring up that speaks it."

"You're running too much to philology, Billy," said Goodwin. " Do you make out the meaning of it?"

" Sure," replied the philosopher of Fortune. " All languages come easy to the man who must know 'em. I've even failed to misunderstand an order to evacuate in classical Chinese when it was backed up by the muzzle of a breech-loader. This little literary essay I hold in my hands means a game of Fox-in-the-Morn-ing. Ever play that, Frank, when you was a kid ?"

" I think so," said Goodwin, laughing. " You join hands all 'round, and —"

"You do not," interrupted Keogh. "You've got a fine sporting game mixed up in your head with * All Around the Rosebush.' The spirit of *Fox-in-the-Morning' is opposed to the holding of hands. I'll tell you how it's played. This president man and his companion in play, they stand up over in San Mateo, ready for the run, and shout: 'Fox-in-the-Morning!' Me and you, standing here, we say: * Goose and the Gander!' They say: 'How many miles is it to London town ?' We say: ' Only a few, if your legs are long enough. How many comes out ? ' They say: 'More than you're able to catch.' And then the game commences."

"I catch the idea," said Goodwin. "It won't do to let the goose and gander slip through our fingers, Billy; their feathers are too valuable. Our crowd is prepared and able to step into the shoes of the government at once; but with the treasury empty we'd stay in power about as long as a tenderfoot would stick on an untamed bronco. We must play the fox on every foot of the coast to prevent their get ting out of the country."

"By the mule-back schedule," said Keogh, "it's five days down from San Mateo. We've got plenty of time to set our outposts. There's only three places on the coast where they can hope to sail from — here and Solitas and Alazan. They're the only points we'll have to guard. It's as easy as a chess problem — fox to play, and mate in three moves. Oh, goosey, goosey, gander, whither do you wander? By the blessing of the literary telegraph the boodle of this benighted fatherland shall be preserved to the honest political party that is seeking to overthrow it."

The situation had been justly outlined by Keogh. The down trail from the capital was at all times a weary road to travel. A jiggety-joggety journey it was; ice-cold and hot, wet and dry. The trail climbed appalling mountains, wound like a rotten string about the brows of breathless precipices, plunged through chilling snow-fed streams, and wrig gled like a snake through sunless forests teeming with menacing insect and animal life. After descending to the foothills it turned to a trident, the central prong ending at Alazan. Another branched off to Coralio; the third penetrated to Solitas. Between the sea and the foothills stretched the five miles breadth of allu vial coast. Here was the flora of the tropics in its rankest and most prodigal growth. Spaces here and there had been wrested from the jungle and planted with bananas and cane and orange groves. The rest was a riot of wild vegetation, the home of monkeys, tapirs, jaguars, alligators and prodigious reptiles and insects. Where no road was cut a serpent could scarcely make its way through the tangle of vines and creepers. Across the treacherous mangrove swamps few things without wings could safely pass. Therefore the fugitives could hope to reach the coast only by one of the routes named.

" Keep the matter quiet, Billy," advised Goodwin. "We don't want the Ins to know that the president is in flight. I suppose Bob's information is something of a scoop in the capital as yet. Otherwise he would not have tried to make his message a confidential one; and, besides, everybody would have heard the news. I'm going around now to see Dr. Zavalla, and start a man up the trail to cut the telegraph wire."

As Goodwin rose, Keogh threw his hat upon the grass by the door and expelled a tremendous sigh.

"What's the trouble, Billy?" asked Goodwin, pausing. "That's the first time I ever heard you sigh."

" Tis the last," said Keogh. " With that sorrow ful puff of wind I resign myself to a life of praise worthy but harassing honesty. What are tintypes, if you please, to the opportunities of the great and hilarious class of ganders and geese? Not that I would be a president, Frank — and the boodle he's got is too big for me to handle — but in some ways I feel my conscience hurting me for addicting myself to photographing a nation instead of running away with it. Frank, did you ever see the ' bundle of mus lin ' that His Excellency has wrapped up and carried off?"

" Isabel Guilbert ?" said Goodwin, laughing. " No, I never did. From what I've heard of her, though, I imagine that she wouldn't stick at anything to carry her point. Don't get romantic, Billy. Sometimes

I begin to fear that there's Irish blood in your ances-try."

"I never saw her either,'* went on Keogh; "but they say she's got all the ladies of mythology, sculp ture, and fiction reduced to chromos. They say she can look at a man once, and he'll turn monkey and climb trees to pick cocoanuts for her. Think of that president man with Lord knows how many hundreds of thousands of dollars in one hand, and this muslin siren in the other, galloping down hill on a sym pathetic mule amid songbirds and flowers! And here is Billy Keogh, because he is virtuous, con demned to the unprofitable swindle of slandering the faces of missing links on tin for an honest living! 'Tis an injustice of nature."

"Cheer up," said Goodwin. "You are a pretty poor fox to be envying a gander. Maybe the en chanting Guilbert will take a fancy to you and your tintypes after we impoverish her royal escort."

"She could do worse," reflected Keogh; "but she won't. 'Tis not a tintype gallery, but the gallery of the gods that she's fitted to adorn She's a very wicked lady, and the president man is in luck. But

I hear Clancy swearing in the back room for having to do all the work." And Keogh plunged for the rear of the " gallery," whistling gaily in a spontaneous way that belied his recent sigh over the questionable good luck of the flying president.

Goodwin turned from the main street into a much narrower one that intersected it at a right angle.

These side streets were covered by a growth of thick, rank grass, which was kept to a navigable shortness by the machetes of the police. Stone side walks, little more than a ledge in width, ran along the base of the mean and monotonous adobe houses. At the outskirts of the village these streets dwindled to nothing; and here were set the palm-thatched huts of the Caribs and the poorer natives, and the shabby cabins of negroes from Jamaica and the West India islands. A few structures raised their heads above the red-tiled roofs of the one-story houses — the bell tower of the Calaboza, the Hotel de los Estranjeros, the residence of the Vesuvius Fruit Company's agent, the store and residence of Bernard Brannigan, a ruined cathedral in which Columbus had once set foot, and, most imposing of all, the Casa Morena —

the summer " White House " of the President of An-churia. On the principal street running along the beach — the Broadway of Coralio — were the larger stores, the government bodega and post-office, the cuartel, the rum-shops and the market place.

On his way Goodwin passed the house of Bernard Brannigan. It was a modern wooden building, two stories in height. The ground floor was occupied by Brannigan's store, the upper one contained the living apartments. A wide, cool porch ran around the house half way up its outer walls. A handsome, vivacious girl neatly dressed in flowing white leaned over the railing and smiled down upon Goodwin. She was no darker than many an Andalusian of high descent; and she sparkled and glowed like a tropical moonlight.

" Good evening, Miss Paula," said Goodwin, taking off his hat, with his ready smile. There was little difference in his manner whether he addressed women or men. Everybody in Coralio liked to re ceive the salutation of the big American.

" Is there any news, Mr. Goodwin ? Please don't say no. Isn't it warm ? I feel just like Mariana in

her moated grange — or was it a range ? — it's hot enough."

" No, there's no news to tell, I believe.," said Good win, with a mischievous look in his eye, " except that old Geddie is getting grumpier and crosser every day. If something doesn't happen to relieve his mind I'll have to quit smoking on his back porch — and there's no other place available that is cool enough."

"He isn't grumpy," said Paula Brannigan, im pulsively, " when he —"

But she ceased suddenly, and drew back with a deepening colour; for her mother had been a mestizo lady, and the Spanish blood had brought to Paula a certain shyness that was an adornment to the other half of her demonstrative nature.

CHAPTER TWO

The Lotus and the Bottle

WILLARD GEDDIE, consul for the United States in Coralio, was working leisurely on his yearly report. Goodwin, who had strolled in as he did daily for a smoke on the much coveted porch, had found him so absorbed in his work that he departed after roundly abusing the consul for his lack of hospitality.

" I shall complain to the civil service department," said Goodwin; —" or is it a depa^jfment ? — per haps it's only a theory. One gets neither civility nor service from you. You won't talk; and you won't set out anything to drink. What kind of a way is that of representing your government ? "

Goodwin strolled out and across to the hotel to see

£8 Cabbages and Kings

if he could bully the quarantine doctor into a game on Coralio's solitary billiard table. His plans were completed for the interception of the fugitives from the capital; and now it was but a waiting game that he had to play.

The consul was interested in his report. He was only twenty-four; and he had not been in Coralio long enough for his enthusiasm to cool in the heat of the tropics — a paradox that may be allowed between Cancer and Capricorn.

So many thousand bunches of bananas, so many thousand oranges and cocoanuts, so many ounces of gold dust, pounds of rubber, coffee, indigo and sar-saparilla — actually, exports were twenty per cent, greater than for the previous year!

A little thrill of satisfaction ran through the consul. Perhaps, he thought, the State Department, upon reading his introduction, would notice — and then he leaned back in his chair and laughed. He was getting as bad as the others. For the moment he had forgotten that Coralio was an insignificant town in an insignificant republic lying along the by-ways of a second-rate sea. He thought of Gregg, the quar-

The Lotus and the Bottle , 29 antine doctor, who subscribed for the London Lancet, expecting to find it quoting his reports to the home Board of Health concerning the yellow fever germ. The consul knew that not one in fifty of his acquaint ances in the States had ever heard of Coralio. He knew that two men, at any rate, would have to read his report — some underling in the State Department and a compositor in the Public Printing Office. Per haps the typesticker would note the increase of com merce in Coralio, and speak of it, over the cheese and beer, to a friend.

He had just written: " Most unaccountable is the supineness of the large exporters in the United States in permitting the French and German houses to practically control the trade interests of this rich and productive country" — when he heard the hoarse notes of a steamer's siren.

Geddie laid down his pen and gathered his Pan ama hat and umbrella. By the sound he knew it to be the Valhalla, one of the line of fruit vessels plying for the Vesuvius Company. Down to ninos of five years, everyone in Coralio could name you each in coming steamer by the note of her siren.

The consul sauntered by a roundabout, shaded way to the beach. By reason of long practice he gauged his stroll so accurately that by the time he arrived on the sandy shore the boat of the customs officials was rowing back from the steamer, which had been boarded and inspected according to the laws of Anchuria.

There is no harbour at Coralio. Vessels of the draught of the Valhalla must ride at anchor a mile from shore. When they take on fruit it is conveyed on lighters and freighter sloops. At Solitas, where there was a fine harbour, ships of many kinds were to be seen, but in the roadstead off Coralio scarcely any save the fruiters paused. Now and then a tramp coaster, or a mysterious brig from Spain, or a saucy French barque would hang innocently for a few days in the offing. Then the custom-house crew would become doubly vigilant and wary. At night a sloop or two would be making strange trips in and out along the shore; and in the morning the stock of Three-Star Hennessey, wines and drygoods in Coralio would be found vastly increased. It has also been said that the customs officials jingled more silver in

the pockets of their red-striped trousers, and that the record books showed no increase in import duties received.

The customs boat and the Valhalla gig reached the shore at the same time. When they grounded in the shallow water there was still five yards of roll ing surf between them and dry sand. Then half-clothed Caribs dashed into the water, and brought in on their backs the Valhalla's purser and the little native officials in their cotton undershirts, blue trou sers with red stripes, and flapping straw hats.

At college Geddie had been a treasure as a first-baseman. He now closed his umbrella, stuck it up right in the sand, and stooped, with his hands resting upon his knees. The purser, burlesquing the pitch er's contortions, hurled at the consul the heavy roll of newspapers, tied with a string, that the steamer always brought for him. Geddie leaped high and caught the roll with a sounding "thwack." The loungers on the beach — about a third of the popula tion of the town — laughed and applauded delight edly. Every week they expected to see that roll of papers delivered and received in that same manner,

and they were never disappointed. Innovations did not flourish in Coralio.

The consul re-hoisted his umbrella, and walked back to the consulate.

This home of a great nation's representative was a wooden structure of two rooms, with a native-built gallery of poles, bamboo and nipa palm running on three sides of it. One room was the official apart ment, furnished chastely with a flat-top desk, a ham mock, and three uncomfortable cane-seated chairs. Engravings of the first and latest president of the country represented hung against the wall. The other room was the consul's living apartment.

It was eleven o'clock when he returned from the beach, and therefore breakfast time. Chanca, the Carib woman who cooked for him, was just serving the meal on the side of the gallery facing the sea — a spot famous as the coolest in Coralio. The break fast consisted of shark's fin soup, stew of land crabs, breadfruit, a broiled iguana steak, aguacates, a freshly cut pineapple, claret and coffee.

Geddie took his seat, and unrolled with luxurious laziness his bundle of newspapers. Here in Coralio

for two days or longer he would read of goings-on in the world very much as we of the world read those whimsical contributions to inexact science that as sume to portray the doings of the Martians. After he had finished with the papers they would be sent on the rounds of the other English-speaking resi dents of the town.

The paper that came first to his hand was one of those bulky mattresses of printed stuff upon which the readers of certain New York journals are sup posed to take their Sabbath literary nap. Opening this the consul rested it upon the table, supporting its weight with the aid of the back of a chair. Then he partook of his meal deliberately, turning the leaves from time to time and glancing half idly at the con tents.

Presently he was struck by something familiar to him in a picture — a half-page, badly printed repro duction of a photograph of a vessel. Languidly in terested, he leaned for a nearer scrutiny and a view of the florid headlines of the column next to the picture.

Yes; he was not mistaken. The engraving was of the eight-hundred-ton yacht Idalia, belonging to

"that prince of good fellows, Midas of the money
market, and society's pink of perfection, J. Ward
Tolliver."

Slowly sipping his black coffee, Geddie read the column of print. Following a listed statement of Mr. Tolliver's real estate and bonds, came a descrip tion of the yacht's furnishings, and then the grain of news no bigger than a mustard seed. Mr. Tolliver, with a party of favoured guests, would sail the next day on a six weeks' cruise along the Central American and South American coasts and among the Bahama Islands. Among the guests were Mrs. Cumberland Payne and Miss Ida Payne, of Norfolk.

The writer, with the fatuous presumption that was demanded of him by his readers, had concocted a romance suited to their palates. He bracketed the names of Miss Payne and Mr. Tolliver until he had well-nigh read the marriage ceremony over them. He played coyly and insinuatingly upon the strings of "on dit" and "Madame Rumour" and "a little bird " and " no one would be surprised," and ended with congratulations.

Geddie, having finished his breakfast, took his pa-

pers to the edge of the gallery, and sat there in his favourite steamer chair with his feet on the bamboo railing. He lighted a cigar, and looked out upon the sea. He felt a glow of satisfaction at finding he was so little disturbed by what he had read. He told himself that he had conquered the distress that had sent him, a voluntary exile, to this far land of the lotus. He could never forget Ida, of course; but there was no longer any pain in thinking about her. When they had had that misunderstanding and quar rel he had impulsively sought this consulship, with the desire to retaliate upon her by detaching himself from her world and presence. He had succeeded thoroughly in that. During the twelve months of his life in Goralio no word had passed between them, though he had sometimes heard of her through the dilatory correspondence with the few friends to whom he still wrote. Still he could not repress a lit tle thrill of satisfaction at knowing that she had not yet married Tolliver or anyone else. But evidently Tolliver had not yet abandoned hope.

Well, it made no difference to him now. He had eaten of the lotus. He was happy and content in

this land of perpetual afternoon. Those old days of life in the States seemed like an irritating dream. He hoped Ida would be as happy as he was The climate as balmy as that of distant Avalon; the fetterless, idyllic round of enchanted days; the life among this indolent, romantic people — a life full of music, flowers, and low laughter; the influence of the imminent sea and mountains, and the many shapes of love and magic and beauty that bloomed in the white tropic nights — with all he was more than content. Also, there was Paula Brannigan.

Geddie intended to marry Paula — if, of course, she would consent; but he felt rather sure that she would do that. Somehow, he kept postponing his proposal. Several times he had been quite near to it; but a mysterious something always held him back. Perhaps it was only the unconscious, instinctive con viction that the act would sever the last tie that bound him to his old world.

He could be very happy with Paula. Few of the native girls could be compared with her. She had attended a convent school in New Orleans for two years; and when she chose to display her accom-

plishments no one could detect any difference be tween her and the girls of Norfolk and Manhattan. But it was delicious to see her at home dressed, as she sometimes was, in the native costume, with bare shoulders and flowing sleeves.

Bernard Brannigan was the great merchant of Coralio. Besides his store, he maintained a train of pack mules, and carried on a lively trade with the interior towns and villages. He had married a na tive lady of high Castilian descent, but with a tinge of Indian brown showing through her olive cheek. The union of the Irish and the Spanish had produced, as it so often has, an offshoot of rare beauty and vari ety. They were very excellent people indeed, and the upper story of their house was ready to be placed at the service of Geddie and Paula as soon as he should make up his mind to speak about it.

By the time two hours were whiled away the consul tired of reading. The papers lay scattered about him on the gallery. Reclining there, he gazed dream ily out upon an Eden. A clump of banana plants interposed their broad shields between him and the gun. The gentle slope from the consulate to the sea

was covered with the dark-green foliage of lemon-trees and orange-trees just bursting into bloom. A lagoon pierced the land like a dark, jagged crystal, and above it a pale ceiba-tree rose almost to the clouds. The waving cocoanut palms on the beach flared their decorative green leaves against the slate of an almost quiescent sea. His senses were cognizant of brilliant scarlets and ochres amid the vert of the coppice, of odours of fruit and bloom and the smoke from Chanca's clay oven under the calabash-tree; of the treble laughter of the native women in their huts, the song of the robin, the salt taste of the breeze, the diminuendo of the faint surf running along the shore — and, gradually, of a white speck, growing to a blur, that intruded itself upon the drab prospect of the sea.

Lazily interested, he watched this blur increase until it became the Idalia steaming at full speed, coming down the coast. Without changing his posi tion he kept his eyes upon the beautiful white yacht as she drew swiftly near, and came opposite to Co-ralio. Then, sitting upright, he saw her float stead ily past and on. Scarcely a mile of sea had separated her from the shore. He had seen the frequent flash of her polished brass work and the stripes of her deck-awnings — so much, and no more. Like a ship on a magic lantern slide the Idalia had crossed the illu minated circle of the consul's little world, and was gone. Save for the tiny cloud of smoke that was left hanging over the brim of the sea, she might have been an immaterial thing, a chimera of his idle brain.

Geddie went into his office and sat down to dawdle over his report. If the reading of the article in the paper had left him unshaken, this silent passing of the Idalia had done for him still more. It had brought the calm and peace of a situation from which all uncertainty had been erased. He knew that men sometimes hope without being aware of it. Now, since she had come two thousand miles and had passed without a sign, not even his unconscious self need cling to the past any longer.

After dinner, when the sun was low behind the mountains, Geddie walked on the little strip of beach under the cocoanuts. The wind was blowing mildly landward, and the surface of the sea was rippled by tiny wavelets.

A 40 Cabbages and Kings

A miniature breaker, spreading with a soft "swish " upon the sand brought with it something round and shiny that rolled back again as the wave receded. The next influx beached it clear, and Geddie picked it up. The thing was a long-necked wine bottle of colourless glass. The cork had been driven in tight ly to the level of the mouth, and the end covered with dark-red sealing-wax. The bottle contained only what seemed to be a sheet of paper, much curled from the manipulation it had undergone while being inserted. In the sealing-wax was the impression of a seal — probably of a signet-ring, bearing the initials of a monogram; but the impression had been hastily made, and the letters were past anything more cer tain than a shrewd conjecture. Ida Payne had always worn a signet-ring in preference to any other finger decoration. Geddie thought he could make out the familiar "I P"; and a queer sen sation of disquietude went over him. More person al and intimate was this reminder of her than had been the sight of the vessel she was doubtless on. He walked back to his house, and set the bcfljle on his desk.

Throwing off his hat and coat, and lighting a lamp — for the night had crowded precipitately upon the brief twilight — he began to examine his piece of sea salvage.

By holding the bottle near the light and turning it judiciously, he made out that it contained a double sheet of note-paper filled with close writing; further, that the paper was of the same size and shade as that always used by Ida; and that, to the best of his be lief, the handwriting was hers. The imperfect glass of the bottle so distorted the rays of light that he could read no word of the writing; but certain capital let ters, of which he caught comprehensive glimpses, were Ida's, he felt sure.

There was a little smile both of perplexity and amusement in Geddie's eyes as he set the bottle down, and laid three cigars side by side on his desk. He fetched his steamer chair from the gallery, and stretched himself comfortably. He would smoke those three cigars while considering the problem.

For it amounted to a problem. He almost wished that he had not found the bottle; but the bottle was there. Why should it have drifted in from the sea, whence come so many disquieting things, to disturb his peace ?

In this dreamy land, where time seemed so redund ant, he had fallen into the habit of bestowing much thought upon even trifling matters.

He began to speculate upon many fanciful theo ries concerning the story of the bottle, rejecting each in turn.

Ships in danger of wreck or disablement some times cast forth such precarious messengers calling for aid. But he had seen the Idalia not three hours before, safe and speeding. Suppose the crew had mutinied and imprisoned the passengers below, and the message was one begging for succour! But, premising such an improbable outrage, would the agitated captives have taken the pains to fill four pages of note-paper with carefully penned arguments to their rescue.

Thus by elimination he soon rid the matter of the more unlikely theories, and was reduced — though aversely — to the less assailable one that the bottle contained a message to himself. Ida knew he was in Corah o; she must have launched the bottle while

the yacht was passing and the wind blowing fairly toward the shore.

As soon as Geddie reached this conclusion a wrin kle came between his brows and a stubborn look set tled around his mouth. He sat looking out through the doorway at the gigantic fire-flies traversing the quiet streets.

If this was a message to him from Ida, what could it mean save an overture toward a reconciliation? And if that, why had she not used the same methods of the post instead of this uncertain and even flippant means of communication ? A note in an empty bot tle, cast into the sea! There was something light and frivolous about it, if not actually contemptuous.

The thought stirred his pride and subdued what ever emotions had been resurrected by the rinding of the bottle.

Geddie put on his coat and hat and walked out. He followed a street that led him along the border of the little plaza where a band was playing and people were rambling, care-free and indolent. Some timorous senoritas scurrying past with fire-flies tangled in the jetty braids of their hair glanced at him with shy, flat-

tering eyes. The air was languorous with the scent of
jasmin and orange-blossoms.

The consul stayed his steps at the house of Bernard Brannigan. Paula was swinging in a hammock on the gallery. She rose from it like a bird from its nest, The colour came to her cheek at the sound of Ged-die's voice.

He was charmed at the sight of her costume — a flounced muslin dress, with a little jacket of white flannel, all made with neatness and style. He sug gested a stroll, and they walked out to the old Indian well on the hill road. They sat on the curb, and there Geddie made the expected but long-deferred speech. Certain though he had been that she would not say him nay, he was thrilled with joy at the com pleteness and sweetness of her surrender. Here was surely a heart made for love and steadfastness. Here was no caprice or questionings or captious stand ards of convention.

When Geddie kissed Paula at her door that night he was happier than he had ever been before. " Here in this hollow lotus land, ever to live and lie reclined" seemed to him, as it has seemed to many mariners, the

best as well as the easiest. His future would be an ideal one. He had attained a Paradise without a ser pent. His Eve would be indeed a part of him, unbe-guiled, and therefore more beguiling. He had made his decision to-night, and his heart was full of serene, assured content.

Geddie went back to his house whistling that finest and saddest love song, " La Golondrina." At the door his tame monkey leaped down from his shelf, chattering briskly. The consul turned to his desk to get him some nuts he usually kept there. Reaching in the half-darkness, his hand struck against the bot tle. He started as if he had touched the cold rotund ity of a serpent.

He had forgotten that the bottle was there.

He lighted the lamp and fed the monkey. Then, very deliberately, he lighted a cigar, and took the bottle in his hand, and walked down the path to the beach.

There was a moon, and the sea was glorious. The breeze had shifted, as it did each evening, and was now rushing steadily seaward.

Stepping to the water's edge, Geddie hurled the un opened bottle far out into the sea. It disappeared for

a moment, and then shot upward twice its length. Geddie stood still, watching it. The moonlight was so bright that he could see it bobbing up and down with the little waves. Slowly it receded from the shore, flashing and turning as it went. The wind was carrying it out to sea. Soon it became a mere speck, doubtfully discerned at irregular intervals; and then the mystery of it was swallowed up by the greater mystery of the ocean. Geddie stood still upon the beach, smoking and looking out upon the water.

" Simon! — Oh, Simon! — wake up there, Simon!" bawled a sonorous voice at the edge of the water.

Old Simon Cruz was a half-breed fisherman and smuggler who lived in a hut on the beach. Out of his earliest nap Simon was thus awakened.

He slipped on his shoes and went outside. Just landing from one of the Valhalla 9 s boats was the third mate of that vessel, who was an acquaintance of Si mon's, and three sailors from the fruiter.

" Go up, Simon," called the mate, " and find Dr. Gregg or Mr. Goodwin or anybody that's a friend to Mr. Geddie, and bring 'em here at once."

" Saints of the skies!" said Simon, sleepily, " noth ing has happened to Mr. Geddie ? "

" He's under that tarpauling, "said the mate, point ing to the boat, "and he's rather more than half drownded. We seen him from the steamer nearly a mile out from shore, swimmin' like mad after a bottle that was floatin' in the water, outward bound. We lowered the gig and started for him. He nearly had his hand on the bottle, when he gave out and went under. We pulled him out in time to save him, maybe; but the doctor is the one to decide that."

"A bottle?" said the old man, rubbing his eyes. He was not yet fully awake. " Where is the bottle ?"

" Driftin' along out there some'eres," said the mate, jerking his thumb toward the sea. " Get on with you, Simon."

CHAPTER THREE

Smith

GrOODWIN and the ardent patriot, Zavalla, took all the precautions that their foresight could contrive to prevent the escape of President Miraflores and his companion. They sent trusted messengers up the coast to Solitas and Alazan to warn the local leaders of the flight, and to instruct them to patrol the water line and arrest the fugitives at all hazards should they reveal themselves in that territory. After this was done there remained only to cover the district about Coralio and await the coming of the quarry. The nets were well spread. The roads were so few, the opportunities for embarkation so limited, and the two or three probable points of exit so well guarded that it would be strange indeed if there should slip

through the meshes so much of the country's dignity, romance, and collateral. The president would, with out doubt, move as secretly as possible, and en deavour to board a vessel by stealth from some secluded point along the shore.

On the fourth day after the receipt of Englehart's telegram the Karlsefin, a Norwegian steamer char tered by the New Orleans fruit trade, anchored off Coralio with three hoarse toots of her siren. The Karlsefin was not one of the line operated by the Vesuvius Fruit Company. She was something of a dilettante, doing odd jobs for a company that was scarcely important enough to figure as a rival to the Vesuvius. The movements of the Karlsefin were dependent upon the state of the market. Sometimes she would ply steadily between the Spanish Main and New Orleans in the regular transport of fruit; next she would be making erratic trips to Mobile or Charleston, or even as far north as New York, according to the distribution of the fruit supply.

Goodwin lounged upon the beach with the usual crowd of idlers that had gathered to view the steamer. Now that President Miraflores might be expected to

reach the borders of his abjured country at any time, the orders were to keep a strict and unrelenting watch. Every vessel that approached the shores might now be considered a possible means of escape for the fugi tives; and an eye was kept even on the sloops and dories that belonged to the sea-going contingent of Coralio. Goodwin and Zavalla moved everywhere, but without ostentation, watching the loopholes of escape.

The customs officials crowded importantly into their boat and rowed out to the Karlsefin. A boat from the steamer landed her purser with his papers, and took out the quarantine doctor with his green umbrella and clinical thermometer. Next a swarm of Caribs began to load upon lighters the thousands of bunches of bananas heaped upon the shore and row them out to the steamer. The Karlsefin had no passenger list, and was soon done with the attention of the authorities. The purser declared that the steamer would remain at anchor until morning, tak ing on her fruit during the night. The Karlsefin had come, he said, from New York, to which port her latest load of oranges and cocoanuts had been con-

veyed. Two or three of the freighter sloops were engaged to assist in the work, for the captain was anxious to make a quick return in order to reap the advantage offered by a certain dearth of fruit in the States.

About four o'clock in the afternoon another of those marine monsters, not very familiar in those waters, hove in sight, following the fateful Idalia — a graceful steam yacht, painted a light buff, clean-cut as a steel engraving. The beautiful vessel hovered off shore, see-sawing the waves as lightly as a duck in a rain barrel. A swift boat manned by a crew in uniform came ashore, and a stocky-built man leaped to the sands.

The new-comer seemed to turn a disapproving eye upon the rather motley congregation of native Anchurians, and made his way at once toward Good win, who was the most conspicuously Anglo-Saxon figure present. Goodwin greeted him with courtesy.

Conversation developed that the newly landed one was named Smith, and that he had come in a yacht. A meagre biography, truly; for the yacht was most apparent; and the "Smith" not beyond a reasonable

guess before the revelation. Yet to the eye of Good win, who had seen several things, there was a dis crepancy between Smith and his yacht. A bullet-headed man Smith was, with an oblique, dead eye and the moustache of a cocktail-mixer. And unless he had shifted costumes before putting off for shore he had affronted the deck of his correct vessel clad in a pearl-gray derby, a gay plaid suit and vaudeville neckwear. Men owning pleasure yachts generally harmonize better with them.

Smith looked business, but he was no advertiser. He commented upon the scenery, remarking upon its fidelity to the pictures in the geography; and then in quired for the United

States consul. Goodwin pointed out the starred-and-striped bunting hanging above the little consulate, which was concealed be hind the orange-trees.

" Mr. Geddie, the consul, will be sure to be there," said Goodwin. " He was very nearly drowned a few days ago while taking a swim in the sea, and the doctor has ordered him to remain indoors for some time."

Smith plowed his way through the sand to the con-sulate, his haberdashery creating violent discord against the smooth tropical blues and greens.

Geddie was lounging in his hammock, somewhat pale of face and languid in pose. On that night when the Valhalla s boat had brought him ashore apparently drenched to death by the sea, Doctor Gregg and his other friends had toiled for hours to preserve the little spark of life that remained to him. The bottle, with its impotent message, was gone out to sea, and the problem that it had provoked was reduced to a simple sum in addition — one and one make two, by the rule of arithmetic; one by the rule of romance.

There is a quaint old theory that man may have two souls — a peripheral one which serves ordinarily, and a central one which is stirred only at certain times, but then with activity and vigour. While under the domination of the former a man will shave, vote, pay taxes, give money to his family, buy subscription books and comport himself on the average plan. But let the central soul suddenly become dominant, and he may, in the twinkling of an eye, turn upon the part ner of his joys with furious execration; he may change

his politics while you could snap your fingers; he may deal out deadly insult to his dearest friend; he may get him, instanter, to a monastery or a dance hall; he may elope, or hang himself — or he may write a song or poem, or kiss his wife unasked, or give his funds to the search of a microbe. Then the pe ripheral soul will return; and we have our safe, sane citizen again. It is but the revolt of the Ego against Order; and its effect is to shake up the atoms only that they may settle where they belong.

Geddie's revulsion had been a mild one — no more than a swim in a summer sea after so inglorious an object as a drifting bottle. And now he was him self again. Upon his desk, ready for the post, was a letter to his government tendering his resignation as consul, to be effective as soon as another could be appointed in his place. For Bernard Bran-nigan, who never did things in a half-way man ner, was to take Geddie at once for a partner in his very profitable and various enterprises; and Paula was happily engaged in plans for refurnish ing and decorating the upper story of the Brannigan house.

The consul rose from his hammock when he saw the conspicuous stranger in his door.

"Keep your seat old man," said the visitor, with an airy wave of his large hand. " My name's Smith; and I've come in a yacht. You are the consul — is that right? A big, cool guy on the beach directed me here. Thought I'd pay my respects to the flag."

"Sit down," said Geddie. "I've been admiring your craft ever since it came in sight. Looks like a fast sailer. What's her tonnage ? "

"Search me!" said Smith. "I don't know what she weighs in at. But she's got a tidy gait. The Rambler — that's her name — don't take the dust of anything afloat. This is my first trip on her. I'm taking a squint along this coast just to get an idea of the countries where the rubber and red pepper and revolutions come from. I had no idea there was so much scenery down here. Why, Central Park ain't in it with this neck of the woods. I'm from New York. They get monkeys, and cocoanuts, and parrots down here — is that right?"

"We have them all," said Geddie. "I'm quite

sure that our fauna and flora would take a prize over Central Park."

" Maybe they would," admitted Smith, cheerfully. "I haven't seen them yet. But I guess you've got us skinned on the animal and vegetation question. You don't have much travel here, do you ? "

" Travel ?" queried the consul. " I suppose you mean passengers on the steamers. No; very few people land in Coralio. An investor now and then — tourists and sight-seers generally go further down the coast to one of the larger towns where there is a har bour. "

" I see a ship out there loading up with bananas," said Smith. " Any passengers come on her ? "

"That's the Karlsefin" said the consul. "She's a tramp fruiter — made her last trip to New York, I believe. No; she brought no passengers. I saw her boat come ashore, and there was no one. About the only exciting recreation we have here is watching steamers when they arrive; and a passenger on one of them generally causes the whole town to turn out. If you are going to remain in Coralio a while, Mr. Smith, I'll be glad to take you around to meet some people. There are four or five American chaps that are good to know, besides the native high-fliers."

"Thanks," said the yachtsman, "but I wouldn't put you to the trouble. I'd like to meet the guys you speak of, but I won't be here long enough to do much knocking around. That cool gent on the beach spoke of a doctor; can you tell me where I could find him? The Rambler ain't quite as steady on her feet as a Broadway hotel; and a fellow gets a touch of seasickness now and then. Thought I'd strike the croaker for a handful of the little sugar pills, in case I need 'em."

"You will be apt to find Dr. Gregg at the hotel," said the consul, " You can see it from the door — it's that two-story building with the balcony, where the orange-trees are."

The Hotel de los Estranjeros was a dreary hostelry, in great disuse both by strangers and friends. It stood at a corner of the Street of the Holy Sepul chre. A grove of small orange-trees crowded against one side of it, enclosed by a low, rock wall over which a tall man might easily step. The house was of plastered adobe, stained a hundred shades of colour by the salt breeze and the sun. Upon its upper bal cony opened a central door and two windows con taining broad jalousies instead of sashes.

The lower floor communicated by two doorways with the narrow, rock-paved sidewalk. The pul-peria — or drinking shop — of the proprietress, Ma-dama Timotea Ortiz, occupied the ground floor. On the bottles of brandy, anisada, Scotch " smoke " and inexpensive wines behind the little counter the dust lay thick save where the fingers of infrequent cus tomers had left irregular prints. The upper story contained four or five guest-rooms which were rarely put to their destined use. Sometimes a fruit-grower, riding in from his plantation to confer with his agent, would pass a melancholy night in the dismal upper story; sometimes a minor native official on some trifling government quest would have his pomp and majesty awed by Madama's sepulchral hospitality. But Madama sat behind her bar content, not desir ing to quarrel with Fate. If anyone required meat, drink or lodging at the Hotel de los Estranjeros they had but to come, and be served. Estd bueno. If they came not, why, then, they came not. Estd bueno.

As the exceptional yachtsman was making his way down the precarious sidewalk of the Street of the Holy Sepulchre, the solitary permanent guest of that decay ing hotel sat at its door, enjoying the breeze from the sea.

Dr. Gregg, the quarantine physician, was a man of fifty or sixty, with a florid face and the longest beard between Topeka and Terra del Fuego. He held his position by virtue of an appointment by the Board of Health of a seaport city in one of the South ern states. That city feared the ancient enemy of every Southern seaport — the yellow fever — and it was the duty of Dr. Gregg to examine crew and pas sengers of every vessel leaving Coralio for prelim inary symptoms. The duties were light, and the salary, for one who lived in Coralio, ample. Surplus time there was in plenty; and the good doctor added to his gains by a large private practice among the residents of the coast. The fact that he did not know ten words of Spanish was no obstacle; a pulse could be felt and a fee collected without one being a linguist. Add to the description the facts that the doctor had a story to tell concerning the operation

of trepanning which no listener had ever allowed him to conclude, and that he believed in brandy as a pro phylactic; and the special points of interest possessed by Dr. Gregg will have become exhausted.

The doctor had dragged a chair to the sidewalk. He was coatless, and he leaned back against the wall and smoked, while he stroked his beard. Surprise came into his pale blue eyes when he caught sight of Smith in his unusual and prismatic clothes.

" You're Dr. Gregg — is that right ? " said Smith, feeling the dog's head pin in his tie. " The constable — I mean the consul, told me you hung out at this caravansary. My name's Smith; and I came in a yacht. Taking a cruise around, looking at the mon keys and pineapple-trees. Come inside and have a drink, Doc. This cafe looks on the blink, but I guess it can set out something wet."

"I will join you, sir, in just a taste of brandy," said Dr. Gregg, rising quickly. "I find that as a prophylactic a little brandy is almost a necessity in this climate."

As they turned to enter the pulperia a native man, barefoot, glided noiselessly up and addressed the

doctor in Spanish. He was yellowish-brown, like an over-ripe lemon; he wore a cotton shirt and rag ged linen trousers girded by a leather belt. His face was like an animal's, live and wary, but without promise of much intelligence. This man jabbered with animation and so much seriousness that it seemed a pity that his words were to be wasted.

Dr. Gregg felt his pulse.

" You sick ? " he inquired.

" Mi mujer estd enferma en la casa" said the man, thus endeavouring to convey the news, in the only language open to him, that his wife lay ill in her palm-thatched hut.

The doctor drew a handful of capsules filled with a white powder from his trousers pocket. He counted out ten of them into the native's hand, and held up his forefinger impressively.

"Take one," said the doctor, "every two hours." He then held up two fingers, shaking them emphati cally before the native's face. Next he pulled out his watch and ran his finger round its dial twice. Again the two fingers confronted the patient's nose. " Two — two — two hours," repeated the doctor.

" Si, Sefior" said the native, sadly.

He pulled a cheap silver watch from his own pocket and laid it in the doctor's hand. " Me bring," said he, struggling painfully with his scant English," other watchy to-morrow." Then he departed down-heart-edly with his capsules.

"A very ignorant race of people, sir," said the doctor, as he slipped the watch into his pocket. "He seems to have mistaken my directions for taking the physic for the fee. However, it is all right. He owes me an account, anyway. The chances are that he won't bring the other watch. You can't depend on anything they promise you. About that drink, now? How did you come to

Coralio, Mr. Smith? I was not aware that any boats except the Karlsefin had arrived for some days."

The two leaned against the deserted bar; and Ma-dama set out a bottle without waiting for the doctor's order. There was no dust on it.

After they had drank twice Smith said:

"You say there were no passengers on the Karl sefin, Doc ? Are you sure about that ? It seems to

me I heard somebody down on the beach say that there was one or two aboard."

"They were mistaken, sir. I myself went out and put all hands through a medical examination, as usual. The Karlsefin sails as soon as she gets her bananas loaded, which will be about daylight in the morning, and she got everything ready this after noon. No, sir, there was no passenger list. Like that Three-Star? A French schooner landed two slooploads of it a month ago. If any customs duties on it went to the distinguished republic of Anchuria you may have my hat. If you won't have another, come out and let's sit in the cool a while. It isn't often we exiles get a chance to talk with somebody from the outside world."

The doctor brought out another chair to the side walk for his new acquaintance. The two seated themselves.

"You are a man of the world," said Dr. Gregg; " a man of travel and experience. Your decision in a matter of ethics and, no doubt, on the points of equity, ability and professional probity should be of value. I would be glad if you will listen to the his-

tory of a case that I think stands unique in medical annals.

" About nine years ago, while I was engaged in the practice of medicine in my native city, I was called to treat a case of contusion of the skull. I made the diagnosis that a splinter of bone was pressing upon the brain, and that the surgical operation known as trepanning was required. However, as the patient was a gentleman of wealth and position, I called in for consultation Dr.—"

Smith rose from his chair, and laid a hand, soft with apology, upon the doctor's shirt sleeve.

"Say, Doc," he said, solemnly, "I want to hear that story. You've got me interested; and I don't want to miss the rest of it. I know it's a loola by the way it begins; and I want to tell it at the next meeting of the Barney O'Flynn Association, if you don't mind. But I've got one or two matters to attend to first. If I get 'em attended to in time I'll come right back and hear you spiel the rest before bedtime — is that right?"

"By all means," said the doctor, "get your busi ness attended to, and then return. I shall wait up

for you. You see, one of the most prominent phy sicians at the consultation diagnosed the trouble as a blood clot; another said it was an abscess, but I —"

"Don't tell me now, Doc. Don't spoil the story. Wait till I come back. I want to hear it as it runs off the reel — is that right ? "

The mountains reached up their bulky shoulders to receive the level gallop of Apollo's homing steeds, the day died in the lagoons and in the shad owed banana groves and in the mangrove swamps, where the great blue crabs were beginning to crawl to land for their nightly ramble. And it died, at last, upon the highest peaks. Then the brief twilight, ephemeral as the flight of a moth, came and went; the Southern Cross peeped with its topmost eye above a row of palms, and the fire-flies heralded with their torches the approach of soft-footed night.

In the offing the Karlsefin swayed at anchor, her lights seeming to penetrate the water to countless fathoms with their shimmering, lanceolate reflec tions. The Caribs were busy loading her by means of the great lighters heaped full from the piles of fruit ranged upon the shore.

On the sandy beach, with his back against a cocoa-nut-tree and the stubs of many cigars lying around him, Smith sat waiting, never relaxing his sharp gaze in the direction of the steamer.

The incongruous yachtsman had concentrated his interest upon the innocent fruiter. Twice had he been assured that no passengers had come to Coralio on board of her. And yet, with a per sistence not to be attributed to an idling voyager, he had appealed the case to the higher court of his own eyesight. Surprisingly like some gay-coated lizard, he crouched at the foot of the cocoa-nut palm, and with the beady, shifting eyes of the selfsame reptile, sustained his espionage on the Karlsefin.

On the white sands a whiter gig belonging to the yacht was drawn up, guarded by one of the white-ducked crew. Not far away in a pulperia on the shore-following Calle Grande three other sailors swag gered with their cues around Coralio's solitary bil liard-table. The boat lay there as if under orders to be ready for use at any moment. There was in the atmosphere a hint of expectation, of waiting

for something to occur, which was foreign to the air of Coralio.

Like some passing bird of brilliant plumage, Smith alights on this palmy shore but to preen his wings for an instant and then to fly away upon silent pinions. When morning dawned there was no Smith, no wait ing gig, no yacht in the offing. Smith left no inti mation of his mission there, no footprints to show where he had followed the trail of his mystery on the sands of Coralio that night. He came; he spake his strange jargon of the asphalt and the cafes; he sat under the cocoanut-tree, and vanished. The next morning Coralio, Smithless, ate its fried plantain and said: "The man of pictured clothing went him self away." With the siesta the incident passed, yawning, into history.

So, for a time, must Smith pass behind the scenes of the play. He comes no more to Coralio nor to Doctor Gregg, who sits in vain, wagging his redund ant beard, waiting to enrich his derelict audience with his moving tale of trepanning and jealousy.

But prosperously to the lucidity of these loose pages, Smith shall flutter among them again. In the

nick of time he shall come to tell us why he strewed so many anxious cigar stumps around the cocoanut palm that night. This he must do; for, when he sailed away before the dawn in his yacht Rambler, he carried with him the answer to a riddle so big and preposterous that few in Anchuria had ven tured even to propound it.

CHAPTER FOUR

Caught

1 HE plans for the detention of the flying President Miraflores and his companion at the coast line seemed hardly likely to fail. Dr. Zavalla himself had gone to the port of Alazan to establish a guard at that point. At Coralio the Liberal patriot Varras could be depended upon to keep close watch. Good win held himself responsible for the district about Coralio.

The news of the president's flight had been dis closed to no one in the coast towns save trusted mem bers of the ambitious political party that was desir ous of succeeding to power. The telegraph wire running from San Mateo to the coast had been cut far up on the mountain trail by an emissary of

Zavalla's. Long before this could be repaired and word received along it from the capital the fugitives would have reached the coast and the question of escape or capture been solved.

Goodwin had stationed armed sentinels at fre quent intervals along the shore for a mile in each direction from Coralio. They were instructed to keep a vigilant lookout during the night to prevent Miraflores from attempting to embark stealthily by means of some boat or sloop found by chance at the water's edge. A dozen patrols walked the streets of Coralio unsuspected, ready to intercept the truant official should he show himself there.

Goodwin was very well convinced that no pre cautions had been overlooked. He strolled about the streets that bore such high-sounding names and were but narrow, grass-covered lanes, lending his own aid to the vigil that had been intrusted to him by Bob Englehart.

The town had begun the tepid round of its nightly diversions. A few leisurely dandies, clad in white duck, with flowing neckties, and swinging slim bam boo canes, threaded the grassy by-ways toward the

houses of their favoured senoritas. Those who wooed the art of music dragged tirelessly at whining concertinaj, or fingered lugubrious guitars at doors and windows. An occasional soldier from the cuar-tel, with flapping straw hat, without coat or shoes, hurried by, balancing his long gun like a lance in one hand. From every density of the foliage the giant tree frogs sounded their loud and irritating clatter. Further out, where the by-ways perished at the brink of the jungle, the guttural cries of marauding bab oons and the coughing of the alligators in the black estuaries fractured the vain silence of the wood.

By ten o'clock the streets were deserted. The oil lamps that had burned, a sickly yellow, at random corners, had been extinguished by some economical civic agent. Coralio lay sleeping camly between top pling mountains and encroaching sea like a stolen babe in the arms of its abductors. Somewhere over in that tropical darkness — perhaps already threading the profundities of the alluvial lowlands — the high adventurer and his mate were moving toward land's end. The game of Fox-in-the-Moming should be coming soon to its close.

Goodwin, at his deliberate gait, passed the long, low cuartel where Coralio's contingent of Anchuria's military force slumbered, with its bare toes pointed heavenward. There was a law that no civilian might come so near the headquarters of that citadel of war after nine o'clock, but Goodwin was always forget ting the minor statutes.

" Quien vive?" shrieked the sentinel, wrestling prodigiously with his lengthy musket.

" Americano, " growled Goodwin, without turning his head, and passed on, unhalted.

To the right he turned, and to the left up the street that ultimately reached the Plaza Nacional. When within the toss of a cigar stump from the intersecting Street of the Holy Sepulchre, he stopped suddenly in the pathway.

He saw the form of a tall man, clothed in black and carrying a large valise, hurry down the cross-street in the direction of the beach. And Goodwin's second glance made him aware of a woman at the man's el bow on the farther side, who seemed to urge forward, if not even to assist, her companion in their swift but silent progress. They were no Coralians, those two<

Goodwin followed at increased speed, but without any of the artful tactics that are so dear to the heart of the sleuth. The American was too broad to feel the instinct of the detective. He stood as an agent for the people of Anchuria, and but for political reasons he would have demanded then and there the money. It was the design of his party to secure the imperilled fund, to restore it to the treasury of the country, and to declare itself in power without bloodshed or resist ance.

The couple halted at the door of the Hotel de los Estranjeros, and the man struck upon the wood with Aie impatience of one unused to his entry being stayed. Madama was long in response; but after a time her light showed, the door was opened, and the guests housed.

Goodwin stood in the quiet street, lighting another cigar. In two minutes a faint gleam began to show between the slats of the jalousies in the upper story of the hotel. " They have engaged rooms," said Good win to himself. "So, then, their arrangements for sailing have yet to be made."

At that moment there came along one Esteban

Delgado, a barber, an enemy to existing govern ment, a jovial plotter against stagnation in any form. This barber was one of Coralio's saddest dogs, often remaining out of doors as late as eleven, post meridian. He was a partisan Liberal; and he greeted Goodwin with flatulent importance as a brother in the cause. But he had something important to tell.

"What think you, Don Frank!" he cried, in the universal tone of the conspirator. " I have to-night shaved la barba — what you call the' weeskers* of the Presidente himself, of this countree! Consider! He sent for me to come. In the poor casita of an old woman he awaited me — in a verree leetle house in a dark place. Carramba I — el Senor Presidente to make himself thus secret and obscured! I think he desired not to be known—but, car a jo! can you shave a man and not see his face ? This gold piece he gave me, and said it was to be all quite still. I think, Don Frank, there is what you call a chip over the bug."

" Have you ever seen President Miraflores before ? " asked Goodwin.

" But once," answered Esteban. "He is tall; and he had weeskers, verree black and sufficient." " Was anyone else present when you shaved him ?" " An old Indian woman, Senor, that belonged with the casa, and one senorita—a ladee of so much beau-tee ! — ah, Dios !"

"All right, Esteban," said Goodwin. "It's very lucky that you happened along with your tonsorial in formation. The new administration will be likely to remember you for this."

Then in a few words he made the barber acquaint ed with the crisis into which the affairs of the nation had culminated, and instructed him to remain out side, keeping watch upon the two sides of the hotel that looked upon the street, and observing whether anyone should attempt to leave the house by any door or window. Goodwin himself went to the door through which the guests had entered, opened it and stepped inside.

Madama had returned downstairs from her jour ney above to see after the comfort of her lodgers. Her candle stood upon the bar. She was about to take a thimbleful of rum as a solace for having her rest dis-

turbed. She looked up without surprise or alarm as her third caller entered.

"Ah! it is the Senor Goodwin. Not often does he honour my poor house by his presence."

"I must come oftener," said Goodwin, with the Goodwin smile. " I hear that your cognac is the best between Belize to the north and Rio to the south. Set out the bottle, Madama, and let us have the proof in un vasito for each of us."

" My aguardiente, " said Madama, with pride, " is the best. It grows, in beautiful bottles, in the dark places among the banana-trees. Si, Senor. Only at midnight can they be picked by sailor-men who bring them, before daylight comes, to your back door. Good aguardiente is a verree difficult fruit to handle, Senor Goodwin."

Smuggling, in Coralio, was much nearer than com petition to being the life of trade. One spoke of it slyly, yet with a certain conceit, when it had been well accomplished.

"You have guests in the house to-night," said Goodwin, laying a silver dollar upon the counter.

" Why not ? " said Madama, counting the change.

" Two; but the smallest while'finished to arrive. One sefior, not quite old, and one senorita of sufficient handsomeness. To their rooms they have ascended, not desiring the to-eat nor the to-drink. Two rooms — Numero 9 and Numero 10."

" I was expecting that gentleman and that lady," said Goodwin. "I have important negocios that must be transacted. Will you allow me to see them?"

"Why not?" sighed Madama, placidly. "Why should not Senor Goodwin ascend and speak to his friends ? Esid bueno. Room Numero 9 and room Numero 10."

Goodwin loosened in his coat pocket the American revolver that he carried, and ascended the steep, dark stairway.

In the hallway above, the saffron light from a hang ing lamp allowed him to select the gaudy numbers on the doors. He turned the knob of Number 9, entered and closed the door behind him.

If that was Isabel Guilbert seated by the table in that poorly furnished room, report had failed to do her charms justice. She rested her head upon one

hand. Extreme fatigue was signified in every line of her figure; and upon her countenance a deep per plexity was written. Her eyes were gray-irised, and of that mould that seems to have belonged to the orbs of all the famous queens of hearts. Their whites were singularly clear and brilliant, concealed above the irises by heavy horizontal lids, and showing a snowy line below them. Such eyes denote great nobility, vigour, and, if you can conceive of it, a most generous selfishness. She looked up when the American en tered, with an expression of surprised inquiry, but without alarm.

Goodwin took off his hat and seated himself, with his characteristic deliberate ease, upon a corner of the table. He held a lighted cigar between his fingers. He took this familiar course because he was sure that preliminaries would be wasted upon Miss Guilbert. He knew her history, and the small part that the con ventions had played in it.

"Good evening," he said. "Now, madame, let us come to business at once. You will observe that I mention no names, but I know who is in the next room, and what he carries in that valise. That is the

point which brings me here. I have come to dictate terms of surrender."

The lady neither moved nor replied, but steadily regarded the cigar in Goodwin's hand.

" We," continued the dictator, thoughtfully regard ing the neat buckskin shoe on his gently swinging foot—"I speak for a considerable majority of the people—demand the return of the stolen funds be longing to them. Our terms go very little further than that. They are very simple. As an accredited spokesman, I promise that our interference will cease if they are accepted. Give up the money, and you and your companion will be permitted to proceed wherever you will. In fact, assistance will be given you in the matter of securing a passage by any out going vessel you may choose. It is on my personal responsibility that I add congratulations to the gen tleman in Number 10 upon his taste in feminine charms."

Returning his cigar to his mouth, Goodwin ob served her, and saw that her eyes followed it and rested upon it with icy and significant concentration. Apparently she had not heard a word he had said.

He understood, tossed the cigar out the window, and, with an amused laugh, slid from the table to his feet.

" That is better," said the lady. " It makes it pos sible for me to listen to you. For a second lesson in good manners, you might now tell me by whom I am being insulted."

" I am sorry," said Goodwin, leaning one hand on the table, "that my time is too brief for devoting much of it to a course of etiquette. Come, now; I appeal to your good sense. You have shown your self, in more than one instance, to be well aware of what is to your advantage. This is an occasion that demands the exercise of your undoubted intelligence. There is no mystery here. I am Frank Goodwin; and I have come for the money. I entered this room at a venture. Had I entered the other I would have had it before now. Do you want it in words ? The gentleman in Number 10 has betrayed a great trust. He has robbed his people of a large sum, and it is I who will prevent their losing it. I do not say who that gentleman is; but if I should be forced to see him and he should prove to be a certain high official of the republic, it will be my duty to arrest him. The house

is guarded. I am offering you liberal terms. It is not absolutely necessary that I confer personally with the gentleman in the next room. Bring me the valise containing the money, and we will call the affair ended."

The lady arose from her chair and stood for a mo ment, thinking deeply.

"Do you live here, Mr. Goodwin?" she asked, presently.

"Yes."

" What is your authority for this intrusion ? "

" I am an instrument of the republic. I was ad vised by wire of the movements of the— gentleman in Number 10."

"May I ask you two or three questions? I be lieve you to be a man more apt to be truthful than — timid. What sort of a town is this — Coralio, I think they call it?"

"Not much of a town," said Goodwin, smiling. " A banana town, as they run. Grass huts, 'dobes, five or six two-story houses, accommodations limited, population half-breed Spanish and Indian, Caribs and blackamoors. No sidewalks to speak of, no

amusements. Rather unmoral. That's an offhand sketch, of course."

"Are there any inducements, say in a social or in a business way, for people to reside here ? "

"Oh, yes," answered Goodwin, smiling broadly. "There are no afternoon teas, no hand-organs, no de partment stores — and there is no extradition treaty."

" He told me," went on the lady, speaking as if to herself, and with a slight frown, "that there were towns on this coast of beauty and importance; that there was a pleasing social order — especially an American colony of cultured residents."

"There is an American colony," said Goodwin, gazing at her in some wonder. " Some of the mem bers are all right. Some are fugitives from justice from the States. I recall two exiled bank presidents, one army paymaster under a cloud, a couple of man-slayers, and a widow — arsenic, I believe, was the sus picion in her case. I myself complete the colony, but, as yet, I have not distinguished myself by any particular crime."

"Do not lose hope," said the lady, dryly; "I see nothing in your actions to-night to guarantee you fur-

ther obscurity. Some mistake has been made; I do not know just where. But him you shall not disturb to-night. The journey has fatigued him so that he has fallen asleep, I think, in his clothes. You talk of stolen money! I do not understand you. Some mistake has been made. I will convince you. Re main where you are and I will bring you the valise that you seem to covet so, and show it to you."

She moved toward the closed door that connected the two rooms, but stopped, and half turned and be stowed upon Goodwin a grave, searching look that ended in a quizzical smile.

"You force my door," she said, "and you follow your ruffianly behaviour with the basest accusations; and yet"— she hesitated, as if to reconsider what she was about to say —" and yet

— it is a puzzling thing — I am sure there has been some mistake."

She took a step toward the door, but Goodwin stayed her by a light touch upon her arm. I have said before that women turned to look at him in the streets. He was the viking sort of man, big, good-looking, and with an air of kindly truculence. She was dark and proud, glowing or pale as her mood

moved her. I do not know if Eve were light or dark, but if such a woman had stood in the garden I know that the apple would have been eaten. This woman was to be Goodwin's fate, and he did not know it; but he must have felt the first throes of destiny, for, as he faced her, the knowledge of what report named her turned bitter in his throat.

" If there has been any mistake," he said, hotly, " it was yours. I do not blame the man who has lost his country, his honour, and is about to lose the poor con solation of his stolen riches as much as I blame you, for, by Heaven! I can very well see how he was brought to it. I can understand, and pity him. It is such women as you that strew this degraded coast with wretched exiles, that make men forget their trusts, that drag—"

The lady interrupted him with a weary gesture.

"There is no need to continue your insults," she said, coldly. "I do not understand what you are saying, nor do I know what mad blunder you are making; but if the inspection of the contents of a gentleman's portmanteau will rid me of you, let us delay it no longer."

She passed quickly and noiselessly into the other room, and returned with the heavy leather valise, which she handed to the American with an air of pa tient contempt.

Goodwin set the valise quickly upon the table and began to unfasten the straps. The lady stood by, with an expression of infinite scorn and weariness upon her face.

The valise opened wide to a powerful, sidelong wrench. Goodwin dragged out two or three articles of clothing, exposing the bulk of its contents — pack age after package of tightly packed United States bank and treasury notes of large denomination. Reckoning from the high figures written upon the paper bands that bound them, the total must have come closely upon the hundred thousand mark.

Goodwin glanced swiftly at the woman, and saw, with surprise and a thrill of pleasure that he wondered at, that she had experienced an unmistakable shock. Her eyes grevs wide, she gasped, and leaned heavily against the table. She had been ignorant, then, he inferred, that her companion had looted the govern ment treasury. But why, he angrily asked himself,

should he be so well pleased to think this wandering and unscrupulous singer not so black as report had painted her?

A noise in the other room startled them both. The door swung open, and a tall, elderly, dark complex-ioned man, recently shaven, hurried into the room.

All the pictures of President Miraflores represent him as the possessor of a luxuriant supply of dark and carefully tended whiskers; but the story of the bar ber, Esteban, had prepared Goodwin for the change.

The man stumbled in from the dark room, his eyes blinking at the lamplight, and heavy from sleep.

"What does this mean?" he demanded in excel lent English, with a keen and perturbed look at the American — " robbery ? "

"Very near it," answered Goodwin. "But I rather think I'm in time to prevent it. I represent the people to whom this money belongs, and I have come to convey it back to them." He thrust his hand into a pocket of his loose, linen coat.

The other man's hand went quickly behind him.

"Don't draw," called Goodwin, sharply; "I've got you covered from my pocket"

The lady stepped forward, and laid one hand upon the shoulder of her hesitating companion, She pointed to the table. "Tell me the truth— the truth," she said, in a low voice. ((Whose money is that?"

The man did not answer. He gave a deep, long-drawn sigh, leaned and kissed her on the forehead, stepped back into the other room and closed the door.

Goodwin foresaw his purpose, and jumped for the door, but the report of the pistol echoed as his hand touched the knob. A heavy fall followed, and some one swept him aside and struggled into the room of the fallen man.

A desolation, thought Goodwin, greater than that derived from the loss of cavalier and gold must have been in the heart of the enchantress to have wrung from her, in that moment, the cry of one turning to the all-forgiving, all-comforting earthly consoler—to have made her call out from that bloody and dishon oured room—"Oh, mother, mother, mother!"

But there was an alarm outside. The barber, Es-tebdn, at the sound of the shot, had raised his voice; and the shot itself had aroused half the town. A pat

tering of feet came up the street, and official orders rang out on the still air. Goodwin had a duty to per form. Circumstances had made him the custodian of his adopted country's treasure. Swiftly cramming the money into the valise, he closed it, leaned far out of the window and dropped it into a thick orange-tree in the little inclosure below.

They will tell you in Coralio, as they delight in tell ing the stranger, of the conclusion of that tragic flight. They will tell you how the upholders of the law came apace when the alarm was sounded — the Comandante in red slippers and a jacket like a head waiter's and girded sword, the soldiers with their in terminable guns, followed by outnumbering officers struggling into their gold lace and epaulettes; the barefooted policemen (the only capables in the lot), and ruffled citizens of every hue and description.

They say that the countenance of the dead man was marred sadly by the effects of the shot; but he was identified as the fallen president by both Goodwin and the barber Esteban. On the next morning mes sages began to come over the mended telegraph wire;

and the story of the flight from the capital was given out to the public. In San Mateo the revolutionary party had seized the sceptre of government, without opposition, and the vivas of the mercurial populace quickly effaced the interest belonging to the unfor tunate Miraflores.

They will relate to you how the new government sifted the towns and raked the roads to find the valise containing Anchuria's surplus capital, which the pres ident was known to have carried with him, but all in vain. In Coralio Senor Goodwin himself led the searching party which combed that town as carefully as a woman combs her hair; but the money was not found.

So they buried the dead man, without honours, back of the town near the little bridge that spans the mangrove swamp; and for a real a boy will show you his grave. They say that the old woman in whose hut the barber shaved the president placed the wooden slab at his head, and burned the inscription upon it with a hot iron.

You will hear also that Senor Goodwin, like a tower of strength, shielded Dona Isabel Guilbert

through those subsequent distressful days; and that his scruples as to her past career (if he had any) van ished; and her adventuresome waywardness (if she had any) left her, and they were wedded and were happy.

The American built a home on a little foot hill near the town. It is a conglomerate structure of na tive woods that, exported, would be worth a fortune, and of brick, palm, glass,'bamboo and adobe. There is a paradise of nature about it; and something of the same sort within. The natives speak of its interior with hands uplifted in admiration. There are floors polished like mirrors and covered with hand-woven Indian rugs of silk fibre, tall ornamenf6 and pictures, musical instruments and papered walls —" figure-it-to-yourself !" they exclaim.

But they cannot tell you in Coralio (as you shall learn) what became of the money that Frank Good win dropped into the orange-tree. But that shall come later; for the palms are fluttering in the breeze, bidding us to sport and gaiety.

CHAPTER FIVE

Cupid's Exile Number Two

1 HE United States of America, after looking over its stock of consular timber, selected Mr. John De Graffenreid Atwood, of Dalesburg, Alabama, for a successor to Willard Geddie, resigned.

Without prejudice to Mr. Atwood, it will have to be acknowledged that, in this instance, it was the man who sought the office. As with the self-ban ished Geddie, it was nothing less than the artful smiles of lovely woman that had driven Johnny At wood to the desperate expedient of accepting office under a despised Federal Government so that he might go far, far away and never see again the false, fair face that had wrecked his young life. The con sulship at Coralio seemed to offer a retreat sufficiently

removed and romantic enough to inject the necessary

drama into the pastoral scenes of Dalesburg life.

It was while playing the part of Cupid's exile that Johnny added his handiwork to the long list of casu alties along the Spanish Main by his famous ma nipulation of the shoe market, and his unparalleled feat of elevating the most despised and useless weed in his own country from obscurity to be a valuable product in international commerce.

The trouble began, as trouble often begins instead of ending, with a romance. In Dalesburg there was a man named Elijah Hemstetter, who kept a general store. His family consisted of one daughter called Rosine, a name that atoned much for "Hemstetter." This young woman was possessed of plentiful attrac tions, so that the young men of the community were agitated in their bosoms. Among the more agitated was Johnny, the son of Judge Atwood, who lived in the big colonial mansion on the edge of Dalesburg.

It would seem that the desirable Rosine should have been pleased to return the affection of an At wood, a name honoured all over the state long before and since the war. It does seem that she should have

Cupid's Exile Number Two 93 gladly consented to have been led into that stately but rather empty colonial mansion. But not so. There was a cloud on the horizon, a threatening, cumulus cloud, in the shape of a lively and shrewd young farmer in the neighbourhood who dared to enter the lists as a rival to the high-born Atwood.

One night Johnny propounded to Rosine a ques tion that is considered of much importance by the young of the human species. The accessories were all there — moonlight, oleanders, magnolias, the mock-bird's song. Whether or no the shadow of Pinkney Dawson, the prosperous young farmer came between them on that occasion is not known; but Rosine's answer was unfavourable. Mr. John De Graffenried Atwood bowed till his hat touched the lawn grass, and went away with his head high, but with a sore wound in his pedigree and heart. A Hemstetter refuse an Atwood! Zounds!

Among other accidents of that year was a Demo cratic president. Judge Atwood was a warhorse of Democracy. Johnny persuaded him to set the wheels moving for some foreign appointment. He would go away — away. Perhaps in years to come

Rosine would think how true, how faithful his love had been, and would drop a tear— maybe in the cream she would be skimming for Pink Dawson's breakfast.

The wheels of politics revolved; and Johnny was appointed consul to Coralio. Just before leaving he dropped in at Hemstetter's to say good-bye. There was a queer, pinkish look about Rosine's eyes; and had the two been alone, the United States might have had to cast about for another consul. But Pink Dawson was there, of course, talking about his 400-acre orchard, and the three-mile alfalfa tract, and the 200-acre pasture. So Johnny shook hands with Rosine as coolly as if he were only going to run up to Montgomery for a couple of days. They had the royal manner when they chose, those Atwoods.

" If you happen to strike anything in the way of a good investment down there, Johnny," said Pink Dawson, " just let me know, will you ? I reckon I could lay my hands on a few extra thousands 'most any time for a profitable deal."

" Certainly, Pink," said Johnny, pleasantly. " If I strike anything of the sort I'll let you in with pleasure."

So Johnny went down to Mobile and took a fruit steamer for the coast of Anchuria.

When the new consul arrived in Coralio the strangeness of the scenes diverted him much. He was only twenty-two; and the grief of youth is not worn like a garment as it is by older men. It has its seasons when it reigns; and then it is unseated for a time by the assertion of the keen senses.

Billy Keogh and Johnny seemed to conceive a mutual friendship at once. Keogh took the new consul about town and presented him to the hand ful of Americans and the smaller number of French and Germans who made up the "foreign" contin gent. And then, of course, he had to be more for mally introduced to the native officials, and have his credentials transmitted through an interpreter.

There was something about the young Southerner that the sophisticated Keogh liked. His manner was simple almost to boyishness; but he possessed the cool carelessness of a man of far greater age and experience. Neither uniforms nor titles, red tape nor foreign languages, mountains nor sea weighed upon his spirits. He was heir to all the ages, an

Atwood, of Dalesburg; and you might know every

thought conceived in his bosom.

Geddie came down to the consulate to explain the duties and workings of the office. He and Keogh tried to interest the new consul in their description of the work that his government expected him to per form.

" It's all right," said Johnny from the hammock that he had set up as the official reclining place. " If anything turns up that has to be done I'll let you fellows do it. You can't expect a Democrat to work during his first term of holding office."

"You might look over these headings," suggested Geddie, "of the different lines of exports you will have to keep account of. The fruit is classified; and there are the valuable woods, coffee, rubber—"

" That last account sounds all right," interrupted Mr. Atwood. " Sounds as if it could be stretched. I want to buy a hew flag, a monkey, a guitar and a barrel of pineapples. Will that rubber account stretch over 'em ? "

"That's merely statistics," said Geddie, smiling. "The expense account is what you want, It is

Cupid's Exile Number Two 97 supposed to have a slight elasticity. The * stationery' items are sometimes carelessly audited by the State Department."

" We're wasting our time," said Keogh. " This man was born to hold office. He penetrates to the root of the art at one step of his eagle eye. The true genius of government shows its hand in every word of his speech."

" I didn't take this job with any intention of work ing," explained Johnny, lazily. "I wanted to go somewhere in the world where they didn't talk about farms. There are none here, are there ? "

" Not the kind you are acquainted with, 1 ' answered the ex-consul. " There is no such art here as agricul ture. There never was a plow or a reaper within the boundaries of Anchuria."

" This is the country for me," murmured the con sul, and immediately he fell asleep.

The cheerful tintypist pursued his intimacy with Johnny in spite of open charges that he did so to obtain a preemption on a seat in that coveted spot, the rear gallery of the consulate. But whether his designs were selfish or purely friendly, Keogh

achieved that desirable privilege. Few were thf nights on which the two could not be found reposing there in the sea breeze, with their heels on the railing, and the cigars and brandy conveniently near.

One evening they sat thus, mainly silent,, for their talk had dwindled before the stilling influence of an unusual night.

There was a great, full moon; and the sea was mother-of-pearl. Almost every sound was hushed, for the air was but faintly stirring; and the town lay panting, waiting for the night to cool. Off-shore lay the fruit steamer Andador, of the Vesuvius line, full-laden and scheduled to sail at six in the morning. There were no loiterers on the beach. So bright was the moonlight that the two men could see the small pebbles shining on the beach where the gentle surf wetted them.

Then down the coast, tacking close to shore, slowly swam a little sloop, white-winged like some snowy sea fowl. Its course lay within twenty points of the wind's eye; so it veered in and out again in long, slow strokes like the movements of a graceful skater.

Again the tactics of its crew brought it close in-

Cupid's Exile Number Two 99 shore, this time nearly opposite the consulate; and then there blew from the sloop clear and surprising notes as if from a horn of elf land. A fairy bugle it might have been, sweet and silvery and unexpected, playing with spirit the familiar air of " Home, Sweet Home."

It was a scene set for the land of the lotus. The authority of the sea and the tropics, the mystery that attends unknown sails, and the prestige of drifting music on moonlit waters gave it an anodynous charm. Johnny Atwood felt it, and thought of Dalesburg; but as soon as Keogh's mind had arrived at a theory concerning the peripatetic solo he sprang to the railing, and his ear-rending yawp fractured the silence of Coralio like a cannon shot.

"Mel-lin-ger a-jioy! "

The sloop was now on its outward tack; but from it came a clear, answering hail:

" Good-bye, Billy . . . go-ing home — bye!"

The Andador was the sloop's destination. No doubt some passenger with a sailing permit from some up-the-coast point had come down in this sloop to catch the regular fruit steamer on its return trip.

Like a coquettish pigeon the little boat tacked on its eccentric way until at last its white sail was lost to sight against the larger bulk of the fruiter's side.

"That's old H. P. Mellinger," explained Keogh, dropping back into his chair. " He's going back to New York. He was private secretary of the late hot-foot president of this groceiy and

fruit stand that they call a country. His job's over now; and I guess old Mellinger is glad."

" Why does he disappear to music, like Zo-zo, the magic queen ? " asked Johnny. " Just to show 'em that he doesn't care ? "

"That noise you heard is a phonograph," said Keogh. "I sold him that. Mellinger had a graft in this country that was the only thing of its kind in the world. The tooting machine saved it for him once, and he always carried it around with him afterward."

"Tell me about it," demanded Johnny, betraying interest.

"I'm no disseminator of narratives," said Keogh. "I can use language for purposes of speech; but when I attempt a discourse the words come out as

Cupid's Exile Number Two 101 they will, and they may make sense when they strike the atmosphere, or they may not."

"I want to hear about that graft," persisted Johnny. " You've got no right to refuse. I've told you all about every man, woman and hitching post in Dalesburg."

" You shall hear it," said Keogh. " I said my in stincts of narrative were perplexed. Don't you be lieve it. It's an art I've acquired along with many other of the graces and sciences."

CHAPTER SIX

The Phonograph and the Graft

VV HAT was this graft?" asked Johnny, with the impatience of the great public to whom tales are told.

" 'Tis contrary to art and philosophy to give you the information," said Keogh, calmly. "The art of narrative consists in concealing from your audience everything it wants to know until after you expose your favourite opinions on topics foreign to the sub ject. A good story is like a bitter pill with the sugar coating inside of it. I will begin, if you please, with a horoscope located in the Cherokee Nation; and end with a moral tune on the phonograph.

"Me and Henry Horsecollar brought the first phonograph to this country. Henry was a quarter-

The Phonograph and the Graft 103 breed, quarter-back Cherokee, educated East in the idioms of football, and West in contraband whisky, and a gentleman, the same as you and me. He was easy and romping in his ways; a man about six foot, with a kind of rubber-tire movement. Yes, he was a little man about five foot five, or five foot eleven. He was what you would call a medium tall man of aver age smallness. Henry had quit college once, and the Muscogee jail three times — the last-named institution on account of introducing and selling whisky in the territories. Henry Horsecollar never let any cigar stores come up and stand behind him. He didn't belong to that tribe of Indians.

"Henry and me met at Texarkana, and figured out this phonograph scheme. He had $360 which came to him out of a land allotment in the reservation. I had run down from Little Rock on account of a distressful scene I had witnessed on the street there. A man stood on a box and passed around some gold watches, screw case, stem-winders, Elgin movement, very elegant. Twenty bucks they cost you over the counter. At three dollars the crowd fought for the tickers. The man happened to find a valise full of

them handy, and he passed them out like putting hot biscuits on a plate. The backs were hard to un screw, but the crowd put its ear to the case, and they ticked mollifying and agreeable. Three of these watches were genuine tickers; the rest were only kickers. Hey ? Why, empty cases with one of them horny black bugs that fly around electric lights in 'em. Them bugs kick off minutes and seconds in dustrious and beautifuL So, this man I was speak ing of cleaned up $288; and then he went away, be cause he knew that when it came time to wind watches in Little Rock an entomologist would be needed, and he wasn't one.

"So, as I say, Henry had $360, and I had $288. The idea of introducing the phonograph to South America was Henry's; but I took to it freely, being fond of machinery of all kinds.

"'The Latin races,' says Henry, explaining easy in the idioms he learned at college, * are peculiarly adapted to be victims of the phonograph. They have the artistic temperament. They yearn for music and color and gaiety. They give wampum to the hand-organ man and the four-legged chicken in the tent

The Phonograph and the Graft 105 when they're months behind with the grocery and the bread-fruit tree.'

" ' Then^' says I, ' we'll export canned music to the Latins; but I'm mindful of Mr. Julius Caesar's account of 'em where he says: " Omnia Gallla in ires paries divisa est ;" which is the same as to say, " We will need all of our gall in devising means to tree them parties."

"I hated to make a show of education; but I was disinclined to be overdone in syntax by a mere Indian, a member of a race to which we owe nothing except the land on which the United States is situated.

" We bought a fine phonograph in Texarkana — one of the best make — and half a trunkful of records. We packed up, and took the T. and P. for New Orleans. From that celebrated centre of molasses and disfranchised coon songs we took a steamer for South America.

"We landed at Solitas, forty miles up the coast from here. 'Twas a palatable enough place to look at. The houses were clean and white; and to look at 'em stuck around among the scenery they re-

minded you of hard-boiled eggs served with lettuce. There was a block of skyscraper mountains in the suburbs; and they kept pretty quiet, like they had crept up there and were watching the town. And the sea was remarking f Sh-sh-sh' on the beach; and now and then a ripe cocoanut would drop ker-blip in the sand; and that was all there was doing. Yes, I judge that town was considerably on the quiet. I judge that after Gabriel quits blowing his horn, and the car starts, with Philadelphia swinging to the last strap, and Pine Gully, Arkansas, hanging onto the rear step, this town of Solitas will wake up and ask if anybody spoke.

"The captain went ashore with us, and offered to conduct what he seemed to like to call the obsequies. He introduced Henry and me to the United States Consul, and a roan man, the head of the Department of Mercenary and Licentious Dispositions, the way it read upon his sign.

"' I touch here again a week from to-day,' says the captain. %

"'By that time,' we told him, 'we'll be amassing wealth in the interior towns with our galvanized

The Phonograph and the Graft 107 prima donna and correct imitations of Sousa's band excavating a march from a tin mine.'

"' Ye'll not,' says the captain. * Ye'll be hypno tized. Any gentleman in the audience who kindly steps upon the stage and looks this country in the eye will be converted to the hypothesis that he's but a fly in the Elgin creamery. Ye'll be standing knee deep in the surf waiting for me, and your machine for making Hamburger steak out of the hitherto re spected art of music will be playing "There's no place like home." !

" Henry skinned a twenty off his roll, and received from the Bureau of Mercenary Dispositions a paper bearing a red seal and a dialect story, and no change.

"Then we got the consul full of red wine, and struck him for a horoscope. He was a thin, youngish kind of man, I should say past fifty, sort of French-Irish in his affections, and puffed up with disconso-lation. Yes, he was a flattened kind of a man, in whom drink lay stagnant, inclined to corpulence and misery. Yes, I think he was a kind of Dutchman, being very sad and genial in his ways.

"' The marvelous invention,' he says,' entitled the
phonograph, has never invaded these shores. The people have never heard it. They would riot believe it if they should. Simple-hearted children of nature, progress has never condemned them to accept the work of a can-opener as an overture, and rag-time might incite them to a bloody revolution. But you can try the experiment. The best chance you have is that the populace may not wake up when you play. There's two ways,' says the consul, * they may take it. They may become inebriated with atten tion, like an Atlanta colonel listening to " Marching Through Georgia," or they will get excited and trans pose the key of the music with an axe and yourselves into a dungeon. In the latter case,' says the consul, * I'll do my duty by cabling to the State Department, and I'll wrap the Stars and Stripes around you when you come to be shot, arid threaten them with the vengeance of the greatest gold export and financial reserve nation on earth. The flag is full of bullet holes now,' says the consul, 'made in that way. Twice before,' says the consul, 'I have cabled our government for a couple of gunboats to protect American citizens. The first time the Department

The Phonograph and the Graft 109 sent me a pair of gum boots. The other time was when a man named Pease was going to be executed here. They referred that appeal to the Secretary of Agriculture. Let us now disturb the sefior behind the bar for a subsequence of the red wine.'

"Thus soliloquized the consul of Solitas to me and Henry Horsecollar.

" But, notwithstanding, we hired a room that after noon in the Calle de los Angeles, the main street that runs along the shore, and put our trunks there. 'Twas a good-sized room, dark and cheerful, but small. 'Twas on a various street, diversified by houses and conservatory plants. The peasantry of the city passed to and fro on the fine pasturage between the sidewalks. 'Twas, for the world, like an opera chorus when the Royal Kafoozlum is about to enter.

"We were rubbing the dust off the machine and getting fixed to start business the next day, when a big, fine-looking white man in white clothes stopped at the door and looked in. We extended the invita tions, and he walked inside and sized us up. He was chewing a long cigar, and wrinkling his eyes,

meditative, like a girl trying to decide which dress
to wear to the party.
;< * New York ?' he says to me finally.
'' Originally, and from time to time,' I says. 'Hasn't it rubbed off yet?'
' * It's simple, 5 says he,' when you know how. It's the fit of the vest. They don't cut vests right any where else.« Coats, maybe, but not vests.'
"The white man looks at Henry Horsecollar and hesitates.
"'Injun,' says Henry; 'tame Injun.'
"'Mellinger,' says the man—'Homer P. Mel-linger. Boys, you're confiscated. You're babes in the wood without a chaperon or referee, and it's my duty to start you going. I'll knock out the props and launch you proper in the pellucid waters of this tropical mud puddle. You'll have to be christened, and if you'll come with me I'll break a bottle of wine across your bows, according to Hoyle.'
"Well, for two days Homer P. Mellinger did the honors. That man cut ice in Anchuria. He was It. He was the Royal Kafoozlum. If me and Henry was babes in the wood, he was a Robin Red-

The Phonograph and the Graft 111 breast from the topmost bough. Him and me and

Henry Horsecollar locked arms, and toted that pho nograph around, and had wassail and diversions. Everywhere we found doors open we went inside and set the machine going, and Mellinger called upon the people to observe the artful music and his two lifelong friends, the Senors Americanos. The opera chorus was agitated with esteem, and followed us from house to house. There was a different kind of drink to be had with every tune. The natives had acquirements of a pleasant think in the way of a drink that gums itself to the recollection. They chop off the end of a green cocoanut, and pour in on the juice of it French brandy and other adjuvants. We had them and other things.

" Mine and Henry's money was counterfeit. Every thing was on Homer P. Mellinger. That man could find rolls of bills concealed in places on his person where Hermann the Wizard couldn't have conjured out a rabbit or an omelette. He could have founded universities, and made orchid collections, and then had enough left to purchase the colored vote of his

Cabbages arid Kings country. Henry and me wondered what his graft was. One evening he told us.

"'Boys/ said he, 'I've deceived you. You think I'm a painted butterfly; but in fact I'm the hardest worked man in this country. Ten years ago I landed on its shores; and two years ago on the point of its jaw. Yes, I guess I can get the decision over this ginger cake commonwealth at the end of any round I choose. I'll confide in you because you are my countrymen and guests, even if you have assaulted my adopted shores with the worst system of noises ever set to music.

"My job is private secretary to the president of this republic; and my duties are running it. I'm not headlined in the bills, but I'm the mustard in the salad dressing just the same. There isn't a law goes before Congress, there isn't a concession granted, there isn't an import duty levied but what H. P. Mellinger he cooks and seasons it. In the front office I fill the president's inkstand and search visit ing statesmen for dirks and dynamite; but in the back room I dictate the policy of the government. You'd never guess in the world how I got my pulL

The Phonograph and the Graft It's the only graft of its kind on earth. I'll put you wise. You remember the old top-liner in the copy book — " Honesty is the Best Policy ? " That's it. I'm working honesty for a graft. I'm the only honest man in the republic. The government knows it; the people know it; the boodlers know it: the foreign investors know it. I make the government keep its faith. If a man is promised a job he gets it. If outside capital buys a concession it gets the goods. I run a monopoly of square dealing here. There's no competition. If Colonel Diogenes were to flash lu's lantern in this precinct he'd have my address in side of two minutes. There isn't big money in it, but it's a sure thing, and lets a man sleep of nights.'

"Thus Homer P. Mellinger made oration to me and Henry Horsecollar. And, later, he divested him self of this remark:

: 'Boys, I'm to hold a soiree this evening with a gang of leading citizens, and I want your assistance. You bring the musical corn sheller and give the affair the outside appearance of a function. There's im portant business on hand, but it musn't show. I can talk to you people. I've been pained for years on ac-

count of not having anybody to blow off and brag to. I get homesick sometimes, and I'd swap the entire perquisites of office for just one hour to have a stein and a caviare sandwich somewhere on Thirty-fourth Street, and stand and watch the street cars go by, and smell the peanut roaster at old Giuseppe's fruit stand.'

" * Yes,' said I,' there's fine caviare at Billy Ren frew's cafe, corner of Thirty-fourth and __'

" 'God knows it,' interrupts Mellinger, 'and if you'd told me you knew Billy Renfrew I'd have in vented tons of ways of making you happy. Billy was my side-kicker in New York. There is a man who never knew what crooked was. Here I am working Honesty for a graft, but that man loses money on it. Carrambos! I get sick at times of this country. Every thing's rotten. From the executive down to the cof fee pickers, they're plotting to down each other and skin their friends. If a mule driver takes off his hat to an official, that man figures it out that he's a popu lar idol, and sets his pegs to stir up a revolution and upset the administration. It's one of my little chores as private secretary to smell out these revolutions and affix the kibosh before they break out and scratch the

The Phonograph and the Graft 115 paint off the government property. That's why I'm down here now in this mildewed coast town. The governor of the district and his crew are plotting to uprise. I've got every one of their names, and they're invited to listen to the phonograph to-night, compli ments of H. P. M. That's the way I'll get them in a bunch, and things are on the programme to happen to them.'

" We three were sitting at table in the cantina of the Purified Saints. Mellinger poured out wine, and was looking some worried; I was thinking.

" ' They're a sharp crowd,' he says, kind of fretful. ' They're capitalized by a foreign syndicate after rub ber, and they're loaded to the muzzle for bribing. I'm sick,' goes on Mellinger,' of comic opera. I want to smell East River and wear suspenders again. At times I feel like throwing up my job, but I'm d—n fool enough to be sort of proud of it. " There's Mellinger," they say here. " POT Dios ! you can't touch him with a million." I'd like to take that record back and show it to Billy Renfrew some day; and that tightens my grip whenever I see a fat thing that I could corral just by winking one eye—and losing my graft. By —,

they can't monkey with me. They know it. What money I get I make honest and spend it. Some day I'll make a pile and go back and eat caviare with Billy. To-night I'll show you how to handle a bunch of corruptionists. I'll show them what Mellinger, private secretary, means when you spell it with the cotton and tissue paper off.'

"Mellinger appears shaky, and breaks his glass against the neck of the bottle.

" I says to myself, * White man, if I'm not mistaken there's been a bait laid out where the tail of your eye could see it.'

"That night, according to arrangements, me and Henry took the phonograph to a room in a 'dobe house in a dirty side street, where the grass was knee high. 'Twas a long room, lit with smoky oil lamps. There was plenty of chairs, and a table at the back end. We set the phonograph on the table. Mellinger was there, walking up and down, disturbed in his predica ments. He chewed cigars and spat 'em out, and he bit the thumb nail of his left hand.

"By and by the invitations to the musieale came sliding in by pairs and threes and spade flushes.

The Phonograph and the Graft 117 Their colour was of a diversity, running from a three-days' smoked meerschaum to a patent-leather polish. They were as polite as wax, being devastated with enjoyments to give Seiior Mellinger the good evenings. I understood their Spanish talk — I ran a pumping engine two years in a Mexican silver mine, and had it pat — but I never let on.

"Maybe fifty of 'em had come, and was seated, when in slid the king bee, the governor of the dis trict. Mellinger met him at the door, and escorted him to the grand stand. When I saw that Latin man I knew that Mellinger, private secretary, had all the dances on his card taken. That was a big, squashy man, the colour of a rubber overshoe, and he had an eye like a head waiter's.

" Mellinger explained, fluent, in the Castilian id ioms, that his soul was disconcerted with joy at in troducing to his respected friends America's greatest invention, the wonder of the age. Henry got the cue and run on an elegant brass-band record and the festivities became initiated. The governor man had a bit of English under his hat, and when the music was choked off he says;

" 'Ver-r-ree fine. Gr-r-r-racias, the American gentleemen, the so esplendeed moosic as to playee.'

" The table was a long one, and Henry and me sat at the end of it next the wall. The governor sat at the other end. Homer P. Mellinger stood at the side of it. I was just wondering how Mellinger was go ing to handle his crowd, when the home talent sud denly opened the services.

"That governor man was suitable for uprisings and policies. I judge he was a ready kind of man, who took his own time. Yes, he was full of attention and immediateness. He leaned his hands on the ta ble and imposed his face toward the secretary man.

" ' Do the American seiiors understand Spanish ?' he asks in his native accents.

"'They do not,' says Mellinger.

"'Then listen/ goes on the Latin man, prompt. 'Themusics are of sufficient prettiness,but not of ne cessity. Let us speak of business. I well know why we are here, since I observe my compatriots. You had a whisper yesterday, Senor Mellinger, of our proposals. To-night we will speak out. We know that you stand in the president's favour, and we know your

The Phonograph and the Graft 119 influence. The government will be changed. We know the worth of your services. We esteem your friendship and aid so much that'— Mellinger raises his hand, but the governor man bottles him up. * Do not speak until I have done.'

" The governor man then draws a package wrap ped in paper from his pocket, and lays it on the table by Mellinger's hand.

" 'In that you will find fifty thousand dollars in money of your country. You can do nothing against us, but you can be worth that for us. Go back to the capital and obey our instructions. Take that money now. We trust you. You will find with it a paper giving in detail the work you will be expected to do for us. Do not have the unwiseness to refuse.'

"The governor man paused, with his eyes fixed on Mellinger, full of expressions and observances. I looked at Mellinger, and was glad Billy Renfrew couldn't see him then. The sweat was popping out on his forehead, and he stood dumb, tapping the little package with the ends of his fingers. The colorado-maduro gang was after his graft. He had only to change his politics, and stuff five figures in his inside pocket.

" Henry whispers to me and wants the pause in the programme interpreted. I whisper back: 'H. P. is up against a bribe, senator's size, and the coons have got him going.' I saw Mellinger's hand moving closer to the package. 'He's weakening,' I whis pered to Henry. ' We'll remind him,' says Henry,' of the peanut-roaster on Thirty-fourth Street, New York.'

" Henry stooped down and got a record from the basketful we'd brought, slid it in the phonograph, and started her off. It was a cornet solo, very neat and beautiful, and the name of it was ' Home, Sweet Home.' Not one of them fifty odd men in the room moved while it was playing, and the governor man kept his eyes steady on Mellinger. I saw Mellinger's head go up little by little, and his hand came creeping away from the package. Not until the last note sounded did anybody stir. And then Homer P. Mel-linger takes up the bundle of boodle and slams it in the governor man's face.

"' That's my answer,' says Mellinger, private sec-

The Phonograph and the Graft retary, * and there'll be another in the morning. I have proofs of conspiracy against every man of you. The show is over, gentlemen.'

is There's one more act,' puts in the governor man. ' You are a servant, I believe, employed by the president to copy letters and answer raps at the door. I am governor here. Senores, I call upon you in the name of the cause to seize this man.'

" That brindled gang of conspirators shoved back their chairs and advanced in force. I could see where Mellinger had made a mistake in massing his enemy so as to make a grand-stand play. I think he made another one, too; but we can pass that, Mellinger's idea of a graft and mine being different, according to estimations and points of view.

"There was only one window and door in that room, and they were in the front end. Here was fifty odd Latin men coming in a bunch to obstruct the leg islation of Mellinger. You may say there were three of us, for me and Henry, simultaneous, declared New York City and the Cherokee Nation in sympathy with the weaker party.

"Then it was that Henry Horsecollar rose to a

Cabbages and Kings point of disorder and intervened, showing, admirable, the advantages of education as applied to the Ameri can Indian's natural intellect and native refinement. He stood up and smoothed back his hair on each side with his hands as you have seen little girls do when they play.

"' Get behind me, both of you,' says Henry.

"'What's it to be, chief?' I asked.

"'I'm going to buck centre/ says Henry, in his football idioms. There isn't a tackle in the lot of them. Follow me close, and rush the game.'

"Then that cultured Red Man exhaled an ar rangement of sounds with his mouth that made the Latin aggregation pause, with thoughtfulness and hesitations. The matter of his proclamation seemed to be a co-operation of the Carlisle war-whoop with the Cherokee college yell. He went at the chocolate team like a bean out of a little boy's nigger shooter. His right elbow laid out the governor man on the gridiron, and he made a lane the length of the crowd so wide that a woman could have carried a step-lad der through it without striking against anything. All Mellinger and me had to do was to follow.

" It took us just three minutes to get out of that street around to military headquarters, where Mel-linger had things his own way. A colonel and a battalion of bare-toed infantry turned out and went back to the scene of the musicale with us, but the conspirator gang was gone. But we recaptured the phonograph with honours of war, and marched back to the cuartel with it playing 'All Coons Look Alike to Me.'

" The next day Mellinger takes me and Henry to one side, and begins to shed tens and twenties.

"'I want to buy that phonograph,' says he. 'I liked that last tune it played at the soiree. 9

" * This is more money than the machine is worth,' says I.

"'Tis government expense money,' says Mellin ger. 'The government pays for it, and it's getting the tune-grinder cheap.'

" Me and Henry knew that pretty well. We knew that it had saved Homer P. Mellinger's graft when he was on the point of losing it; but we never let him. know we knew it.

**' Now you boys better slide off further down the

coast for a while/ says Mellinger,' till I get the screws put on these fellows here. If you don't they'll give you trouble. And if you ever happen to see Billy Renfrew again before I do, tell him I'm coming back to New York as soon as I can make a stake—.honest.'

" Me and Henry laid low until the day the steamer came back. When we saw the captain's boat on the beach we went down and stood in the edge of the water. The captain grinned when he saw us.

" I told you you'd be waiting,' he says. ' Where's the Hamburger machine ?'

" * It stays behind,' I says,' to play " Home, Sweet Home.'"

"'I told you so,' says the captain again. * Climb in the boat.'

"And that," said Keogh, "is the way me and Henry Horsecollar introduced the phonograph into this country. Henry went back to the States, but I've been rummaging around in the tropics ever since They say Mellinger never travelled a mile after that without his phonograph. I guess it kept him reminded about his graft whenever he saw the siren voice of the boodler tip him the wink with a bribe in its hand."

The Phonograph and the Graft 125 " I suppose he's taking it home with him as a sou venir," remarked the consul.

"Not as a souvenir," said Keogh. "He'll need two of 'em in New York, running day and night."

CHAPTER SEVEN Money Maze

1 HE new administration of Anchuria entered upon its duties and privileges with enthusiasm. Its first act was to send an agent to Coralio with impera tive orders to recover, if possible, the sum of money ravished from the treasury by the ill-fated Miraflores.

Colonel Emilio Falcon, the private secretary of Lo-sada, the new president, was despatched from the cap ital upon this important mission.

The position of private secretary to a tropical presi dent is a responsible one. He must be a diplomat, a spy, a ruler of men, a body-guard to his chief, and a smeller-out of plots and nascent revolutions. Often he is the power behind the throne, the dictator of pol-

icy; and a president chooses him with a dozen times the care with which he selects a matrimonial mate.

Colonel Falcon, a handsome and urbane gentle man of Castilian courtesy and debonnaire manners, came to Coralio with the task before him of striking upon the cold trail of the lost money. There he con ferred with the military authorities, who had received instructions to co-operate with him in the search.

Colonel Falcon established his headquarters in one of the rooms of the Casa Morena. Here for a week he held informal sittings — much as if he were a kind of unified grand jury — and summoned before him all those whose testimony might illumine the financial tragedy that had accompanied the less momentous one of the late president's death.

Two or three who were thus examined, among whom was the barber Esteban, declared that they had identified the body of the president before its burial.

" Of a truth," testified Esteban before the mighty secretary, "it was he, the president. Consider! — how could I shave a man and not see his face ? He sent for me to shave him in a small house. He had a

beard very black and thick. Had I ever seen the president before ? Why not ? I saw him once ride forth in a carriage from the vapor in Solitas. When I shaved him he gave me a gold piece, and said there was to be no talk. But I am a Liberal— I am de voted to my country — and I spake of these things to Senor Goodwin."

"It is known," said Colonel Falcon, smoothly, '* that the late President took with him an American leather valise, containing a large amount of money. Did you see that?"

" De veras — no," Esteban answered. " The light in the little house was but a small lamp by which I could scarcely see to shave the President. Such a thing there may have been, but I did not see it. No. Also in the room was a young lady — a señorita of much beauty — that I could see even in so small a light. But the money, senor, or the thing in which it was carried — that I did not see."

The comandante and other officers gave testimony that they had been awakened and alarmed by the noise of a pistol-shot in the Hotel de los Estranjeros. Hurrying thither to protect the peace and dignity of

the republic, they found a man lying dead, with a pistol clutched in his hand. Beside him was a young woman, weeping sorely. Senor Goodwin was also in the room when they entered it. But of the valise of money they saw nothing.

Madame Timotea Ortiz, the proprietress of the hotel in which the game of Fox-in-the-Morning had been played out, told of the coming of the two guests to her house.

" To my house they came," said she —" one senor, not quite old, and one senorita of sufficient handsome ness. They desired not to eat or to drink — not even of my aguardiente, which is the best. To their rooms they ascended — Numero Nueve and Numero Diez. Later came Senor Goodwin, who ascended to speak with them. Then I heard a great noise like that of a canon, and they said that the pobre Presidente had shot himself. Está bueno. I saw nothing of money or of the thing you call veliz that you say he carried it in."

Colonel Falcon soon came to the reasonable con clusion that if anyone in Coralio could furnish a clue to the vanished money, Frank Goodwin must be the

man. But the wise secretary pursued a different course in seeking information from the American. Goodwin was a powerful friend to the new adminis tration, and one who was not to be carelessly dealt with in respect to either his honesty or his courage. Even the private secretary of His Excellency hesitated to have this rubber prince and mahogany baron haled before him as a common citizen of Anchuria. So he sent Goodwin a flowery epistle, each word-petal dripping with honey, requesting the favour of an in terview. Goodwin replied with an invitation to din ner at his own house.

Before the hour named the American walked over to the Gasa Morena, and greeted his guest frankly and friendly. Then the two strolled, in the cool of the afternoon, to Goodwin's home in the environs.

The American left Colonel Falcon in a big, cool, shadowed room with a floor of inlaid and polished woods that any millionaire in the States would have envied, excusing himself for a few minutes. He crossed a patio, shaded with deftly arranged awnings and plants, and entered a long room looking upon the sea in the opposite wing of the house. The broad

jalousies were opened wide, and the ocean breeze flowed in through the room, an invisible current of coolness and health. Goodwin's wife sat near one of the windows, making a water-color sketch of the af ternoon seascape.

Here was a woman who looked to be happy. And more — she looked to be content. Had a poet been inspired to pen just similes concerning her favour, he would have likened her full, clear eyes, with their white-encircled, gray irises, to moonflowers. With none of the goddesses whose traditional charms-have become coldly classic would the discerning rhyme ster have compared her. She was purely Paradisaic, not Olympian. If you can imagine Eve, after the eviction, beguiling the flaming warriors and serenely re-entering the Garden, you will have her. Just so human, and still so harmonious with Eden seemed Mrs. Goodwin.

When her husband entered she looked up, and her lips curved and parted; her eyelids fluttered twice or thrice — a movement remindful (Poesy forgive us!) of the tail-wagging of a faithful dog — and a little ripple went through her like the commotion set up in a weeping willow by a puff of wind. Thus she ever acknowledged his coming, were it twenty times a day. If they who sometimes sat over their wine in Coralio, reshaping old, diverting stories of the madcap career of Isabel Guilbert, could have seen the wife of Frank Goodwin that afternoon in the estimable aura of her happy wifehood, they might have disbelieved, or have agreed to forget, those graphic annals of the life of the one for whom their president gave up his country and his honour.

" I have brought a guest to dinner, " said Goodwin. " One Colonel Falcon, from San Mateo. He is come on government business. I do not think you will care to see him, so I prescribe for you one of those convenient and indisputable feminine headaches."

" He has come to inquire about the lost money, has he not?" asked Mrs. Goodwin, going on with her sketch.

"A good guess!" acknowledged Goodwin. "He has been holding an inquisition among the natives for three days. I am next on his list of witnesses, but as he feels shy about dragging one of Uncle Sam's subjects before him, he consents to give it the outward appearance of a social function. He will apply the torture over my own wine and provender. "

"Has he found anyone who saw the valise of money ? "

"Not a soul. Even Madama Ortiz, whose eyes are so sharp for the sight of a revenue official, does not remember that there was any baggage. "

Mrs. Goodwin laid down her brush and sighed.

" I am so sorry, Frank," she said, *' that they are giving you so much trouble about the money. But we can't let them know about it, can we ? "

" Not without doing our intelligence a great injus tice, " said Goodwin, with a smile and a shrug that he had picked up from the natives. "Americano, though I am, they would have me in the calaboza in half an hour if they knew we had appropriated that valise. No; we must appear as ignorant about the money as the other ignoramuses in Coralio."

" Do you think that this man they have sent sus pects you ?" she asked, with a little pucker of her brows.

" He'd better not," said the American, carelessly. " It's lucky that no one caught a sight of the valise ex-

cept myself. As I was in the rooms when the shot was fired, it is not surprising that they should want to investigate my part in the affair rather closely. But there's no cause for alarm. This colonel is down on the list of events for a good dinner, with a dessert of American ' bluff' that will end the matter, I think."

Mrs. Goodwin rose and walked to the window. Goodwin followed and stood by her side. She leaned to him, and rested in the protection of his strength, as she had always rested since that dark night on which he had first made himself her tower of refuge. Thus they stood for a little while.

Straight through the lavish growth of tropical branch and leaf and vine that confronted them had been cunningly trimmed a vista, that ended at the cleared environs of Coralio, on the banks of the man grove swamp. At the other end of the aerial tunnel they could see the grave and wooden headpiece that bore the name of the unhappy President Miraflores. From this window when the rains forbade the open, and from the green and shady slopes of Goodwin's fruitful lands when the skies were smiling, his wife was wont to look upon that grave with a gentle

sadness that was now scarcely a mar to her happi ness.

" I loved him so, Frank!" she said, " even after that terrible flight and its awful ending. And you have been so good to me, and have made me so happy. It has all grown into such a strange puzzle. If they were to find out that we got the money do you think they would force you to make the amount good to the government ? "

" They would undoubtedly try," answered Good win. " You are right about its being a puzzle. And it must remain a puzzle to Falcon and all his coun trymen until it solves itself. You and I, who know more than anyone else, only know half of the solution. We must not let even a hint about this money get abroad. Let them come to the theory that the presi dent concealed it in the mountains during his journey, or that he found means to ship it out of the country before he reached Coralio. I don't think that Fal con suspects me. He is making a close investigation, according to his orders, but he will find out nothing."

Thus they spake together. Had anyone over heard or overseen them as they discussed the lost

funds of Anchuria there would have been a second puzzle presented. For upon the faces and in the bearing of each of them was visible (if countenances are to be believed) Saxon honesty and pride and hon ourable thoughts. In Goodwin's steady eye and firm lineaments, moulded into material shape by the in ward spirit of kindness and generosity and courage, there was nothing reconcilable with his words.

As for his wife, physiognomy championed her even in the face of their accusive talk. Nobility was in her guise; purity was in her glance. The devotion that she manifested had not even the appearance of that feeling that now and then inspires a woman to share the guilt of her partner out of the pathetic greatness of her love. No, there was a discrepancy here between what the eye would have seen and the ear have heard.

Dinner was served to Goodwin and his guest in the patio, under cool foliage and flowers. The American begged the illustrious secretary to excuse the absence of Mrs. Goodwin, who was suffering, he said, from a headache brought on by a slight calentura.

After the meal they lingered, according to the cus tom, over their coffee and cigars. Colonel Falcon,

with true Castilian delicacy, waited for his host to open the question that they had met to discuss. He had not long to wait. As soon as the cigars were lighted, the American cleared the way by inquiring whether the secretary's investigations in the town had furnished him with any clue to the lost funds.

" I have found no one yet," admitted Colonel Fal con, " who even had sight of the valise or the money. Yet I have persisted. It has been proven in the capi tal that President Miraflores set out from San Mateo with one hundred thousand dollars belonging to the government, accompanied by Seftorita Isabel Guil-bert, the opera singer. The Government, officially and personally, is loathe to believe," concluded Col onel Falcon, with a smile, " that our late President's tastes would have permitted him to abandon on the route, as excess baggage, either of the desirable arti cles with which his flight was burdened."

" I suppose you would like to hear what I have to say about the affair," said Goodwin, coming directly to the point. " It will not require many words.

" On that night, with others of our friends here, I was keeping a lookout for the president, having been

notified of his flight by a telegram in our national cipher from Englehart, one of our leaders in the capi tal. About ten o'clock that night I saw a man and a woman hurrying along the streets. They went to the Hotel de los Estranjeros, and engaged rooms. I fol lowed them upstairs, leaving Esteban, who had come up, to watch outside. The barber had told me that he had shaved the beard from the president's face that night; therefore I was prepared, when I entered the rooms, to find him with a smooth face. When I apprehended him in the name of the people he drew a pistol and shot himself instantly. In a few minutes many officers and citizens were on the spot. I sup pose you have been informed of the subsequent facts."

Goodwin paused. Losada's agent maintained an attitude of waiting, as if he expected a continuance.

" And now," went on the American, looking stead ily into the eyes of the other man, and giving each word a deliberate emphasis, "you will oblige me by attending carefully to what I have to add. I saw no valise or receptacle of any kind, or any money be longing to the Republic of Anchuria. If President Miraflores decamped with any funds belonging to the

treasury of this country, or to himself, or to anyone else, I saw no trace of it in the house or elsewhere, at that time or at any other. Does that statement cover the ground of the inquiry you wished to make of me ? "

Colonel Falcon bowed, and described a fluent curve with his cigar. His duty was performed. Goodwin was not to be disputed He was a loyal supporter of the government, and enjoyed the full confidence of the new president. His rectitude had been the capital that had brought him fortune in An-churia, just as it had formed the lucrative " graft" of Mellinger, the secretary of Miraflores.

" I thank you, Senor Goodwin," said Falcon, " for speaking plainly. Your word will be sufficient for the president. But, Serlor Goodwin, I am instructed to pursue every clue that presents itself in this matter. There is one that I have not yet touched upon. Our friends in France, senor, have a saying, * Cherchez la femmc,' when there is a mystery without a clue. But here we do not have to search. The woman who ac companied the late President in his flight must surely—"

" I must interrupt you there," interposed Goodwin.

" It is true that when I entered the hotel for the pur pose of intercepting President Miraflores I found a lady there. I must beg of you to remember that that lady is now my wife. I speak for her as I do for my self. She knows nothing of the fate of the valise or of the money that you are seeking. You will say to his excellency that I guarantee her innocence. I do not need to add to you, Colonel Falcon, that I do not care to have her questioned or disturbed."

Colonel Falcon bowed again.

"Por supuesto y no!" he cried. And to indicate that the inquiry was ended he added: "And now, senor, let me beg of you to show me that sea view from your galeria of which you spoke. I am a lover of the sea."

In the early evening Goodwin walked back to the town with his guest, leaving him at the corner of the Calle Grande. As he was returning homeward one " Beelzebub " Blythe, with the air of a courtier and the outward aspect of a scarecrow, pounced upon him hopefully from the door of a pulperia.

Blythe had been re-christened " Beelzebub " as an acknowledgment of the greatness of his fall. Once,

in some distant Paradise Lost, he had foregathered with the angels of the earth. But Fate had hurled him headlong down to the tropics, where flamed in his bosom a fire that was seldom quenched. In Cora-lio they called him a beachcomber; but he was, in reality, a categorical idealist who strove to anamor-phosize the dull verities of Me by the means of brandy and rum. As Beelzebub, himself, might have held in his clutch with unwitting tenacity his harp or crown during his tremendous fall, so his namesake had clung to his gold-rimmed eyeglasses as the only souvenir of his lost estate. These he wore with impres-siveness and distinction while he combed beaches and extracted toll from his friends. By some mysterious means he kept his drink-reddened face always smooth ly shaven. For the rest he sponged gracefully upon whomsoever he could for enough to keep him pretty drunk, and sheltered from the rains and night dews. " Hallo, Goodwin!" called the derelict, airily. " I was hoping I'd strike you. I wanted to see you par ticularly. Suppose we go where we can talk. Of course you know there's^a chap down here looking up the money old Miraflores lost."

" Yes," said Goodwin," I've been talking with him. Let's go into Espada's place. I can spare you ten minutes."

They went into the pulperia and sat at a little table upon stools with rawhide tops.

" Have a drink ? " said Goodwin.

"They can't bring it too quickly," said Blythe. " I've been in a drought ever since morning. Hi — muchacho / — el aguardiente por oca. "

" Now, what do you want to see me about ? " asked Goodwin, when the drinks were before them.

"Confound it, old man," drawled Blythe, "why do you spoil a golden moment like this with business ? I wanted to see you — well, this has the preference." He gulped down his brandy, and gazed longingly into the empty glass.

"Have another?" suggested Goodwin.

"Between gentlemen," said the fallen angel, "I don't quite like your use of that word ' another.' It isn't quite delicate. But the concrete idea that the word represents is not displeasing."

The glasses were refilled. Blythe sipped blissfully from his, as he began to enter the state of a true idealist

"I must trot along in a minute or two," hinted Goodwin. "Was there anything in particular?"

Blythe did not reply at once.

" Old Losada would make it a hot country," he re marked at length, " for the man who swiped that grip sack of treasury boodle, don't you think ? "

" Undoubtedly, he would," agreed Goodwin calmly, as he rose leisurely to his feet. " I'll be run ning over to the house now, old man. Mrs. Good win is alone. There was nothing important you had to say, was there ? "

" That's all," said Blythe. " Unless you wouldn't mind sending in another drink from the bar as you go out. Old Espada has closed my account to profit and loss. And pay for the lot, will you, like a good fellow?"

"All right," said Goodwin. " Buenas noches."

"Beelzebub" Blythe lingered over his cups, pol ishing his eyeglasses with a disreputable handker chief.

"I thought I could do it, but I couldn't," he muttered to himself after a time. "A gentleman can't blackmail the man that he drinks with.'*

CHAPTER EIGHT

The Admiral

INFILLED milk draws few tears from an Anchurian administration. Many are its lacteal sources; and the clocks' hands point forever to milking time. Even the rich cream skimmed from the treasury by the be witched Miraflores did not cause the newly-installed patriots to waste time in unprofitable regrets. The government philosophically set about supplying the deficiency by increasing the import duties and by "suggesting" to wealthy private citizens that con tributions according to their means would be con sidered patriotic and in order. Prosperity was expected to attend the reign of Losada, the new president. The ousted office-holders and military favourites organized a new "Liberal" party, and

began to lay their plans for a re-succession. Thus the game of Anchurian politics began, like a Chinese comedy, to unwind slowly its serial length. Here and there Mirth peeps for an instant from the wings and illumines the florid lines.

A dozen quarts of champagne in conjunction with an informal sitting of the president and his cabinet led to the establishment of the navy and the appoint ment of Felipe Carrera as its admiral.

Next to the champagne the credit of the appoint ment belongs to Don Sabas Placido, the newly con firmed Minister of War.

The president had requested a convention of his cabinet for the discussion of questions politic and for the transaction of certain routine matters of state. The session had been signally tedious; the business and the wine prodigiously dry. A sudden, prankish humour of Don Sabas, impelling him to the deed, spiced the grave affairs of state with a whiff of agree able playfulness.

In the dilatory order of business had come a bulle tin from the coast department of Orilla del Mar reporting the seizure by the custom-house officers

at the town of Coralio of the sloop Estrella del Noche and her cargo of drygoods, patent medicines, granu lated sugar and three-star brandy. Also six Martini rifles and a barrel of American whisky. Caught in the act of smuggling, the sloop with its cargo was now, according to law, the property of the republic.

The Collector of Customs, in making his report, departed from the conventional forms so far as to suggest that the confiscated vessel be converted to the use of the government. The prize was the first capture to the credit of the department in ten years. The collector took opportunity to pat his depart ment on the back.

It often happened that government officers re quired transportation from point to point along the coast, and means were usually lacking. Further more, the sloop could be manned by a loyal crew and employed as a coast guard to discourage the per nicious art of smuggling. The collector also ven tured to nominate one to whom the charge of the boat could be safely intrusted — a young man of Coralio, Felipe Carrera — not, be it understood, one

of extreme wisdom, but loyal and the best sailor along the coast.

It was upon this hint that the Minister of War acted, executing a rare piece of drollery that so en livened the tedium of executive session.

In the constitution of this small, maritime banana republic was a forgotten section that provided for the maintenance of a navy. This provision — with many other wiser ones — had lain inert since the establishment of the republic. Anchuria had no navy and had no use for one. It was characteristic of Don Sabas — a man at once merry, learned, whimsical and audacious — that he should have dis turbed the dust of this musty and sleeping statute to increase the humour of the world by so much as a smile from his indulgent colleagues.

With delightful mock seriousness the Minister of War proposed the creation of a navy. He argued its need and the glories it might achieve with such gay and witty zeal that the travesty overcame with its humour even the swart dignity of President Losada himself.

The champagne was bubbling trickily in the veins

of the mercurial statesmen. It was not the custom of the grave governors of Anchuria to enliven their sessions with a beverage so apt to cast a veil of dis paragement over sober affairs. The wine had been a thoughtful compliment tendered by the agent of the Vesuvius Fruit Company as a token of amicable relations — and certain consummated deals — be tween that company and the republic of Anchuria.

The jest was carried to its end. A formidable, official document was prepared, encrusted with chro matic seals and jaunty with fluttering ribbons, bear ing the florid signatures of state. This commission conferred upon el Sefior Don Felipe Carrera the title of Flag Admiral of the Republic of Anchuria. Thus within the space of a few minutes and the dominion of a dozen *' extra dry," the country took its place among the naval powers of the world, and Felipe Carrera became entitled to a salute of nineteen guns whenever he might enter port.

The southern races are lacking in that particular kind of humour that finds entertainment in the defects and misfortunes bestowed by Nature. Ow ing to this defect in their constitution they are not

moved to laughter (as are their northern brothers) by the spectacle of the deformed, the feeble-minded or the insane.

Felipe Carrera was sent upon earth with but half his wits. Therefore, the people of

Coralio called him " El pobrecito loco " — " the poor little crazed one "—-saying that God had sent but half of him to earth, retaining the other half.

A sombre youth, glowering, and speaking only at the rarest times, Felipe was but negatively "loco." On shore he generally refused all conversation. He seemed to know that he was badly handicapped on land, where so many kinds of understanding are needed; but on the water his one talent set him equal with most men. Few sailors whom God had care fully and completely made could handle a sailboat as well. Five points nearer the wind than the best of them he could sail his sloop. When the elements raged and set other men to cowering, the deficiencies of Felipe seemed of little importance. He was a perfect sailor, if an imperfect man. He owned no boat, but worked among the crews of the schooners and sloops that skimmed the coast, trading and

freighting fruit out to the steamers where there was no harbour. It was through his famous skill and boldness on the sea, as well as for the pity felt for his mental imperfections, that he was recommended by the collector as a suitable custodian of the captured sloop.

When the outcome of Don Sabas 5 little pleasantry arrived in the form of the imposing and preposterous commission, the collector smiled. He had not ex pected such prompt and overwhelming response to his recommendation. He despatched a muchacho at once to fetch the future admiral.

The collector waited in his official quarters. His office was in the Calle Grande, and the sea breezes hummed through its windows all day. The col lector, in white linen and canvas shoes, philandered with papers on an antique desk. A parrot, perched on a pen rack, seasoned the official tedium with a fire of choice Castilian imprecations. Two rooms open ed into the collector's. In one the clerical force of young men of variegated complexions transacted with glitter and parade their several duties. Through the open door of the other room could be seen a bronze babe, guiltless of clothing, that rollicked upon the floor. In a grass hammock a thin woman, tinted a pale lemon, played a guitar and swung contentedly in the breeze. Thus surrounded by the routine of his high duties and the visible tokens of agreeable domesticity, the collector's heart was further made happy by the power placed in his hands to brighten the fortunes of the "innocent," Felipe.

Felipe came and stood before the collector. He was a lad of twenty, not ill-favoured in looks, but \t;ith an expression of distant and pondering vacuity. Hv> wore white cotton trousers, down the seams of which he had sewed red stripes with some vague aim at military decoration. A flimsy blue shirt fell open t»t his throat; his feet were bare; he held in his hand the cheapest of straw hats from the States.

" Seil)r Carrera," said the collector, gravely, pro ducing the showy commission, " I have sent for you at the president's bidding. This document that I present to you confers upon you the title of Admiral of this great republic, and gives you absolute com mand of the naval forces and fleet of our country. You may think, friend Felipe, that we have no navy — but yes! The sloop the Estrella del Noehe,, that my brave men captured from the coast smug glers, is to be placed under your command. The boat is to be devoted to the services of your country. You will be ready at all times to convey officials of the government to points along the coast where they may be obliged to visit. You will also act as a coast guard to prevent, as far as you may be able, the crime of smuggling. You will uphold the honour and pres tige of your country at sea, and endeavour to place Anchuria among the proudest naval powers of the world. These are your instructions as the Minister of War desires me to convey them to you. Par Dios / I do not know how all this is to be accom plished, for not one word did his letter contain in respect to a crew or to the expenses of this navy. Per haps you are to provide a crew yourself, Sef :>r Ad miral — I do not know — but it is a very high honour that has descended upon you. I now hand -you your commission. When you are ready for the boat I will give orders that she shall be made ov-'.r into your charge. That is as far as my instructions go." Felipe took the commission that the collector

handed to him. He gazed through the open window at the sea for a moment, with his customary expres sion of deep but vain pondering. Then he turned without having spoken a word, and walked swiftly away through the hot sand of the street.

"Pobrecito loco!" sighed the collector; and the parrot on the pen racks creeched " Loco! — loco! — loco!"

The next morning a strange procession filed through the streets to the collector's office. At its head was the admiral of the navy. Somewhere Felipe had raked together a pitiful semblance of a military uniform — a pair of red trousers, a dingy blue s hort jacket heavily ornamented with gold braid, and an old fatigue cap that must have been cast away by one of the British soldiers in Belize and brouglt away by Felipe on one of his coasting voy ages, iiuckled around his waist was an ancient ship's cutlass contributed to his equipment by Pedro Lafitte, the baker, who proudly asserted its inheri tance from his ancestor, the illustrious buccaneer. At the admiral's heels tagged his newly-shipped crew — three grinning, glossy, black Caribs, bare to the waist, the sand spurting in showers from the spring of their naked feet.

Briefly and with dignity Felipe demanded his vessel of the collector. And now a fresh honour awaited him. The collector's wife, who played the guitar and read novels in the hammock all day, had more than a little romance in her placid, yellow bosom. She had found in an old book an engraving of a flag that purported to be the naval flag of An-churia. Perhaps it had so been designed by the founders of the nation; but, as no navy had ever been established, oblivion had claimed the flag. Labo riously with her own hands she had made a flag after the pattern — a red cross upon a blue-and- white ground. She presented it to Felipe with these words : " Brave sailor, this flag is of your country. Be true, and defend it with your life. Go you with G >d."

For the first time since his appointment the ad miral showed a flicker of emotion. He took the silken emblem, and passed his hand reverently over its surface. "I am the admiral," he said to the collector's lady. Being on land he could bring him self to no more exuberant expression of sentiment

At sea with the flag at the masthead of his navy, some more eloquent exposition of feelings might be forthcoming.

Abruptly the admiral departed with his crew. For the next three days they were busy giving the Estrella del Noche a new coat of white paint trimmed with blue. And then Felipe further adorned him self by fastening a handful of brilliant parrot's plumes in his cap. Again he tramped with his faith ful crew to the collector's office and formally notified him that the sloop's name had been changed to El National.

During the next few months the navy had its trou bles. Even an admiral is perplexed to know what to do without any orders. But none came. Neither did any salaries. El Nacional swung idly at anchor.

When Felipe's little store of money was exhausted he went to the collector and raised the question of finances.

"Salaries!" exclaimed the collector, with hands raised; "Valgame Dios ! not one centavo of my own pay have I received for the last seven months. The pay of an admiral, do you ask ? Quien sabe ? Should

it be less than three thousand pesos? Mira! you will see a revolution in this country very soon. A good sign of it is when the government calls all the time for pesos, pesos, pesos, and pays none out."

Felipe left the collector's office with a look almost of content on his sombre face. A revolution would mean righting, and then the government would need his services. It was rather humiliating to be an admiral without anything to do, and have a hungry crew at your heels begging for reales to buy plantains and tobacco with.

When he returned to where his happy-go-lucky Caribs were waiting they sprang up and saluted, as he had drilled them to do.

"Come, muchachos," said the admiral; "it seems that the government is poor. It has no money to give us. We will earn what we need to live upon. Thus will we serve our country. Soon " — his heavy eyes almost lighted up — " it may gladly call upon us for help."

Thereafter El National turned out with the other coast craft and became a wage-earner. She worked with the lighters freighting bananas and oranges out

to the fruit steamers that could not approach nearer than a mile from the shore. Surely a self-supporting navy deserves red letters in the budget of any nation.

After earning enough at freighting to keep himself and his crew in provisions for a week Felipe would anchor the navy and hang about the little telegraph office, looking like one of the chorus of an insolvent comic opera troupe besieging the manager's den. A hope for orders from the capital was always in his heart. That his services as admiral had never been called into requirement hurt his pride and patriotism. At every call he would inquire, gravely and expect antly, for despatches. The operator would pretend to make a search, and then reply:

"Not yet, it seems, Senor el Almirante — poco tiempo 1 "

Outside in the shade of the lime-trees the crew chewed sugar cane or slumbered, well content to serve a country that was contented with so little service.

One day in the early summer the revolution pre dicted by the collector flamed out suddenly. It had long been smouldering. At the first note of alarm the

admiral of the navy force and fleet made all sail for a larger port on the coast of a neighbouring republic, where he traded a hastily collected cargo of fruit for its value in cartridges for the five Martini rifles, the only guns that the navy could boast. Then to the telegraph office sped the admiral. Sprawling in his favourite corner, in his fast-decaying uniform, with his prodigious sabre distributed between his red legs, he waited for the long-delayed, but now soon expected, orders.

"Not yet, Senw el Almirante" the telegraph clerk would call to him — " poco tiempo ! "

At the answer the admiral would plump himself down with a great rattling of scabbard to await the infrequent tick of the little instrument on the table.

"They will come," would be his unshaken reply; * I am the admiral."

CHAPTER NINE The Flag Paramount

A.T the head of the insurgent party appeared that Hector and learned Theban of the southern re publics, Don Sabas Placido. A traveller, a soldier, a poet, a scientist, a statesman and a connoisseur — the wonder was that he could content himself with the petty, remote life of his native country.

-"It is a whim of Placido's," said a friend who knew him well, " to take up political intrigue. It is not otherwise than as if he had come upon a new tempo in music, a new bacillus in the air, a new scent, or rhyme, or explosive. He will squeeze this revolu tion dry of sensations, and a week afterward will forget it, skimming the seas of the world in his brigantine to add to his already world-famous col-

lections. Collections of what ? Por Dios ! of every thing from postage stamps to prehistoric stone idols."

But, for a mere dilettante, the aesthetic Placido seemed to be creating a lively row. The people admired him; they were fascinated by his brilliancy and flattered by his taking an interest in so small a thing as his native country. They rallied to the call of his lieutenants in the capital, where (somewhat contrary to arrangements) the army remained faith ful to the government. There was also lively skir mishing in the coast towns. It was rumoured that the revolution was aided by the Vesuvius Fruit Com pany, the power that forever stood with chiding smile and uplifted ringer to keep Anchuria in the class of good children. Two of its steamers, the Traveler and the Salvador, were known to have conveyed in surgent troops from point to point along the coast.

As yet there had been no actual uprising in Co-ralio. Military law prevailed, and the ferment was bottled for the time. And then came the word that everywhere the revolutionists were encountering de feat. In the capital the president's forces triumphed;

and there was a rumour that the leaders of the revolt had been forced to fly. hotly pursued.

In the little telegraph office at Coralio there was always a gathering of officials and loyal citizens, awaiting news from the seat of government. One morning the telegraph key began clicking, and pres ently the operator called, loudly: " One telegram for el Almirante, Don Senor Felipe Carrera!"

There was a shuffling sound, a great rattling of tin scabbard, and the admiral, prompt at his spot of waiting, leaped across the room to receive it.

The message was handed to him. Slowly spelling it out, he found it to be his first official order — thus running:

"Proceed immediately with your vessel to mouth of Rio Ruiz; transport beef and provisions to bar racks at Alforan. Martinez, General."

Small glory, to be sure, in this, his country's first call. But it had called, and Joy surged in the ad miral's breast. He drew his cutlass belt to another buckle hole, roused his dozing crew, and in a quarter of an hour El Nacional was tacking swiftly down coast in a stiff landward breeze.

The Rio Ruiz is a small river, emptying into the sea ten miles below Coralio. That portion of the coast is wild and solitary. Through a gorge in the Cordilleras rushes the Rio Ruiz, cold and bubbling, to glide, at last, with breadth and leisure, through an alluvial morass into the sea.

In two hours El Nacional entered the river's mouth. The banks were crowded with a disposition of formidable trees. The sumptuous undergrowth of the tropics overflowed the land, and drowned itself in the fallow waters. Silently the sloop entered there, and met a deeper silence. Brilliant with greens and ochres and floral scarlets, the umbrageous mouth of the Rio Ruiz furnished no sound or move ment save of the sea-going water as it purled against the prow of the vessel. Small chance there seemed of wresting beef or provisions from that empty soli tude.

The admiral decided to cast anchor, and, at the chain's rattle, the forest was stimulated to instant and resounding uproar. The mouth of the Rio Ruiz had only been taking a morning nap.

Parrots and baboons screeched and barked in the trees; a
whirring and a hissing and a booming marked the awakening of animal life; a dark blue
bulk was visible for an instant, as a startled tapir fought his way through the vines.

The navy, under orders, hung in the mouth of the little river for hours. The crew served
the dinner of shark's fin soup, plantains, crab gumbo and sour wine. The admiral, with a three-
foot telescope, closely scanned the impervious foliage fifty yards away.

It was nearly sunset when a reverberating " hallo-o-o!" came from the forest to their left.
It was an swered; and three men, mounted upon mules, crashed through the tropic tangle to
within a dozen yards of the river's bank. There they dismounted; and one, unbuckling his belt,
struck each mule a violent blow with his sword scabbard, so that they, with a fling of heels,
dashed back again into the forest.

Those were strange-looking men to be conveying beef and provisions. One was a large
and exceed ingly active man, of striking presence. He was of the purest Spanish type, with
curling, gray-besprin kled, dark hair, blue, sparkling eyes, and the pro-
nounced air of a caballero grande. The other two were small, brown-faced men, wearing
white mili tary uniforms, high riding boots and swords. The clothes of all were drenched,
bespattered and rent by the thicket. Some stress of circumstance must have driven them, (Liable
a quatre, through flood, mire and jungle.

"O-he! Senior Almirante" called the large man. " Send to us your boat."

The dory was lowered, and Felipe, with one of the Caribs, rowed toward the left bank.

The large man stood near the water's brink, waist deep in the curling vines. As he gazed
upon the scarecrow figure in the stern of the dory a sprightly interest beamed upon his mobile
face.

Months of wageless and thankless service had dimmed the admiral's splendour. His red
trousers were patched and ragged. Most of the bright but tons and yellow braid were gone from
his jacket. The visor of his cap was torn, and depended almost to his eyes. The admiral's feet
were bare.

"Dear admiral," cried the large man, and his voice was like a blast from a horn, " I kiss
your hands

I knew we could build upon your fidelity. You had our despatch — from General
Martinez. A little nearer with your boat, dear Admiral. Upon these devils of shifting vines we
stand with the smallest security."

Felipe regarded him with a stolid face.

" Provisions and beef for the barracks at Alforan," he quoted.

"No fault of the butchers, Almirante mio, that the beef awaits you not. But you are come
in time to save the cattle. Get us aboard your vessel, señor, at once. You first, caballeros — a
priesa! Come back for me. The boat is too small/'

The dory conveyed the two officers to the sloop, and returned for the large man.

" Have you so gross a tiling as food, good admi ral ? " he cried, when aboard. " And,
perhaps, coffee ? Beef and provisions! Nombre de Dios I a little longer and we could have eaten
one of those mules that you, Colonel Rafael, saluted so feelingly with your sword scabbard at
parting. Let us have food; and then we will sail — for the barracks at Alforan — no ? "

The Caribs prepared a meal, to which the three
passengers of El National set themselves with fam ished delight. About sunset, as was its
custom, the breeze veered and swept back from the mountains, cool and steady, bringing a taste
of the stagnant lagoons and mangrove swamps that guttered the low lands. The mainsail of the

sloop was hoisted and swelled to it, and at that moment they heard shouts and a waxing clamour from the bosky profundities of the shore.

" The butchers, my dear admiral," said the large man, smiling, " too late for the slaughter. "

Further than his orders to his crew, the admiral was saying nothing. The topsail and jib were spread, and the sloop glided out of the estuary. The large man and his companions had bestowed them selves with what comfort they could about the bare deck. Belike, the thing big in their minds had been their departure from that critical shore; and now that the hazard was so far reduced their thoughts were loosed to the consideration of further deliverance. But when they saw the sloop turn and fly up coast again they relaxed, satisfied with the course the admiral had taken.

The large man sat at ease, his spirited blue eye en gaged in the contemplation of the navy's commander. He was trying to estimate this sombre and fantastic lad, whose impenetrable stolidity puzzled him. Him self a fugitive, his life sought, and chafing under the smart of defeat and failure, it was characteristic of him to transfer instantly his interest to the study of a thing new to him. It was like him, too, to have con ceived and risked all upon this last desperate and mad cap scheme—this message to a poor, crazed fanatico cruising about with his grotesque uniform and his far cical title. But his companions had been at their wits' end; escape had seemed incredible; and now he was pleased with the success of the plan they had called crack-brained and precarious.

The brief, tropic twilight seemed to slide swiftly into the pearly splendour of a moonlit night. And now the lights of Coralio appeared, distributed against the darkening shore to their right. The admiral stood, silent, at the tiller; the Caribs, like black pan thers, held the sheets, leaping noiselessly at his short commands. The three passengers were watching intently the sea before them, and when at length they

came in sight of the bulk of a steamer lying a mile out from the town, with her lights radiating deep into the water, they held a sudden voluble and close-headed converse. The sloop was speeding as if to strike mid way between ship and shore.

The large man suddenly separated from his com panions and approached the scarecrow at the helm.

" My dear admiral," he said " the government has been exceedingly remiss. I feel all the shame for it that only its ignorance of your devoted service has prevented it from sustaining. An inexcusable over sight has been made. A vessel, a uniform and a crew worthy of your fidelity shall be furnished you. But just now, dear admiral, there is business of moment afoot. The steamer lying there is the Salvador. I and my friends desire to be conveyed to her, where we are sent on the government's business. Do us the favour to shape your course accordingly."

Without replying, the admiral gave a sharp com mand, and put the tiller hard to port. El National swerved, and headed straight as an arrow's course for the shore.

" Do me the favour," said the large man, a trifle res-

lively, " to acknowledge, at least, that you catch the sound of my words." It was possible that the fellow might be lacking in senses as well as intellect.

The admiral emitted a croaking, harsh laugh, and spake.

" They will stand you," he said, " with your face to a wall and shoot you dead. That is the way they kill traitors. I knew you when you stepped into my boat. I have seen your picture in a book. You are Sabas Placido, traitor to your country. With your face to a wall. So, you will die. I am the admiral, and I will take you to them. With your face to a wall. Yes."

Don Sabas half turned and waved his hand, with a ringing laugh, toward his fellow fugitives. " To you, caballeroSy I have related the history of that session when we issued that O! so ridiculous commission. Of a truth our jest has been turned against us. Behold the Frankenstein's monster we have created!"

Don Sabas glanced toward the shore. The lights of Coralio were drawing near. He could see the beach, the warehouse of the Bodega National, the

long, low cuartel occupied by the soldiers, and, behind that, gleaming in the moonlight, a stretch of high adobe wall. He had seen men stood with their faces to that wall and shot dead.

Again he addressed the extravagant figure at the helm.

" It is true," he said, " that I am fleeing the coun try. But, receive the assurance that I care very little for that. Courts and camps everywhere are open to Sabas Placido. Vaya ! what is this molehill of a re public — this pig's head of a country — to a man like me? I am a paisano of everywhere. In Rome, in London, in Paris, in Vienna, you will hear them say: 'Welcome back, Don Sabas.' Come! — tonto — baboon of a boy — admiral, whatever you call your self, turn your boat. Put us on board the Salvador, and here is your pay — five hundred pesos in money of the Estados Unidos — more than your lying government will pay you in twenty years."

Don Sabas pressed a plump purse against the youth's hand. The admiral gave no heed to the words or the movement. Braced against the helm, he was holding the sloop dead on her shoreward

course. His dull face was lit almost to intelligence by some inward conceit that seemed to afford him joy, and found utterance in another parrot-like cackle.

" That is why they do it," he said —" so that you will not see the guns. They fire — boom! — and you fall dead. With your face to the wall. Yes."

The admiral called a sudden q|der to his crew. The lithe, silent Caribs made fast the sheets they held, and slipped down the hatchway into the hold of the sloop. When the last one had disappeared, Don Sabas, like a big, brown leopard, leaped for ward, closed and fastened the hatch and stood, smiling.

" No rifles, if you please, dear admiral," he said. "It was a whimsey of mine once to compile a dic tionary of the Carib lengua. So, I understood your order. Perhaps now you will — "

He cut short his words, for he heard the dull "swish" of iron scraping along tin. The admiral had drawn the cutlass of Pedro Lafitte, and was dart ing upon him. The blade descended, and it was only by a display of surprising agility that the large man

escaped, with only a bruised shoulder, the glancing weapon. He was drawing his pistol as he sprang, and the next instant he shot the admiral down.

Don Sabas stooped over him, and rose again.

"In the heart," he said briefly. "Senores, the navy is abolished."

Colonel Rafael sprang to the helm, and the other officer hastened to loose the mainsail sheets. The boom swung round; El Nacional veered and began to tack industriously for the Salvador.

"Strike that flag, senor," called Colonel Rafael. " Our friends on the steamer will wonder why we are sailing under it."

" Well said," cried Don Sabas. Advancing to the mast he lowered the flag to the deck, where lay its too loyal supporter. Thus ended the Minister of War's little piece of after-dinner drollery, and by the same hand that began it.

Suddenly Don Sabas gave a great cry of joy, and ran down the slanting deck to the side of

Colonel Ra fael. Across his arm he carried the flag of the extin guished navy.

"Mire I mire ! senor. Ah, Dios ! Already can I hear

that great bear of an Oestreicher shout, (Du hast mein herz gebroclien!' Mire! Of my friend, Herr Grunitz, of Vienna, you have heard me relate. That man has travelled to Ceylon for an orchid — to Patagonia for a headdress — to Benares for a slipper — to Mo 1 zambique for a spearhead to add to his famous collec tions. Thou knowest, also, amigo Rafael, that I have been a gatherer of curios. My collection of battle flags of the world's navies was the most complete in existence until last year. Then Herr Grunitz secured two, O! such rare specimens. One of a Barbary state, and one of the Makarooroos, a tribe on the west coast of Africa. I have not those, but they can be procured. But this flag, senor — do you know what it is ? Name of God! do you know ? See that red cross upon the blue and white ground! You never saw it before ? Seguramente no. It is the naval flag of your country. Mire! This rotten tub we stand upon is its navy — that dead cockatoo lying there was its commander — that stroke of cutlass and single pistol shot a sea battle. All a piece of absurd foolery, I grant you — but authentic. There has never been another flag like this, and there never will be another.

No. It is unique in the whole world. Yes. Think of what that means to a collector of flags! Do you know, Coronet mio, how many golden crowns Herr Grunitz would give for this flag ? Ten thousand, likely. Well, a hundred thousand would not buy it. Beautiful flag! Only flag! Little devil of a most heaven-born flag! O-he ! old grumbler beyond the ocean. Wait till Don Sabas comes again to the Konigin Strasse. He will let you kneel and touch the folds of it with one finger. O-he ! old spectacled ran-s acker of the world!"

Forgotten was the impotent revolution, the danger, the loss, the gall of defeat. Possessed solely by the inordinate and unparalleled passion of the collector, he strode up and down the little deck, clasping to his breast with one hand the paragon of a flag. He snap ped his fingers triumphantly toward the east. He shouted the paean to his prize in trumpet tones, as though he would make old Grunitz hear in his musty den beyond the sea.

They were waiting, on the Salvador, to welcome them. The sloop came close alongside the steamer where her sides were sliced almost to the lower deck

for the loading of fruit. The sailors of the Salvador grappled and held her there.

Captain McLeod leaned over the side.

" Well, seiior, the jig is up, I'm told."

" The jig is up ? " Don Sabas looked perplexed for a moment. "That revolution — ah, yes!" With a shrug of his shoulders he dismissed the matter.

The captain learned of the escape and the im prisoned crew.

"Caribs?" he said; "no harm in them." He slipped down into the sloop and kicked loose the hasp of the hatch. The black fellows came tum bling up, sweating but grinning.

"Hey! black boys!" said the captain, in a dialect of his own; " you sabe, catchy boat and vamos back same place quick."

They saw him point to themselves, the sloop and Coralio." Yas, yas!" they cried, with broader grins and many nods.

The four — Don Sabas, the two officers and the captain — moved to quit the sloop. Don Sabas lagged a little behind, looking at the still form of the late admiral, sprawled in his paltry trappings.

" Pobrecito loco," he said softly.

He was a brilliant cosmopolite and a cognoscente of high rank; but, after all, he was of the same race and blood and instinct as this people. Even as the simple paisanos of Coralio had said it, so said Don Sabas. Without a smile, he looked, and said, " The poor little crazed one!"

Stooping he raised the limp shoulders, drew the priceless and induplicable flag under them and over the breast, pinning it there with the diamond star of the Order of San Carlos that he took from the collar of his own coat.

He followed after the others, and stood with them upon the deck of the Salvador. The sailors that steadied El Nacional shoved her off. The jabbering Caribs hauled away at the rigging; the sloop headed for the shore.

And Herr Grunitz's collection of naval flags was still the finest in the world.

CHAPTER TEN

The Shamrock and the Palm

night when there was no breeze, and Co-ralio seemed closer than ever to the gratings of Avernus, five men were grouped about the door of the photograph establishment of Keogh and Clancy. Thus, in all the scorched and exotic places of the earth, Caucasians meet when the day's work is done to preserve the fulness of their heritage by the asper sion of alien things.

Johnny Atwood lay stretched upon the grass in the undress uniform of a Carib, and prated feebly of cool water to be had in the cucumber-wood pumps of Dalesburg. Dr. Gregg, through the prestige of his whiskers and as a bribe against the relation of his im minent professional tales, was conceded the hammock

that was swung between the door jamb and a cala bash-tree. Keogh had moved out upon the grass a little table that held the instrument for burnishing completed photographs. He was the only busy one of the group. Industriously from between the cylin ders of the burnisher rolled the finished depictments of Coralio's citizens. Blanchard, the French mining engineer, in his cool linen viewed the smoke of his cig arette through his calm glasses, impervious to the heat. Clancy sat on the steps, smoking his short pipe. His mood was the gossip's; the others were reduced, by the humidity, to the state of disability desirable in an audience.

Clancy was an American with an Irish diathesis and cosmopolitan proclivities. Many businesses had claimed him, but not for long. The roadster's blood was in his veins. The voice of the tintype was but one of the many callings that had wooed him upon so many roads. Sometimes he could be persuaded to oral construction of his voyages into the informal and egregious. To-night there were symptoms of divulge-ment in him.

"'Tis elegant weather for filibusterin'," he vol-

unteered. " It reminds me of the time I struggled to liberate a nation from the poisonous breath of a ty rant's clutch. 'Twas hard work, 'Tis strainin' to the back and makes corns on the hands."

" I didn't know you had ever lent your sword to an oppressed people," murmured Atwood, from the grass.

"I did," said Clancy; "and they turned it into a ploughshare."

" What country was so fortunate as to secure your aid ? " airily inquired Blanchard.

"Where's Kamchatka?" asked Clancy, with seeming irrelevance.

" Why, off Siberia somewhere in the Arctic re gions, " somebody answered, doubtfully.

" I thought that was the cold one," said Clancy, with a satisfied nod. "I'm always gettin' the two names mixed. 'Twas Guatemala, then — the hot one — I've been filibusterin' with. Ye'll find that country on the map. 'Tis in the district known as the tropics. By the foresight of Providence, it lies on the coast so the geography man could run the names of the towns off into the water. They're an inch long,

small type, composed of Spanish dialects, and, 'tis my opinion, of the same system of syntax that blew up the Maine. Yes, 'twas that country I sailed against, sin gle-handed, and endeavoured to liberate it from a tyrannical government with a single-barreled pickaxe, unloaded at that. Ye don't understand, of course. 'Tis a statement demandin' elucidation and apolo gies.

"'Twas in New Orleans one morning about the first of June; I was standin' down on the wharf, lookin' about at the ships in the river. There was a little steamer moored right opposite me that seemed about ready to sail. The funnels of it were throwin' out smoke, and a gang of roustabouts were carryin' aboard a pile of boxes that was stacked up on the wharf. The boxes were about two feet square, and somethin' like four feet long, and they seemed to be pretty heavy.

" I walked over, careless, to the stack of boxes. I saw one of them had been broken in handlin'. 'Twas curiosity made me pull up the loose top and look in side. The box was packed full of Winchester rifles. * So, so,' says I to myself; * somebody's gettin' a twist

The Shamrock and the Palm 181 on the neutrality laws. Somebody's aidin' with mu nitions of war. I wonder where the popguns are goin'?'

" I heard somebody cough, and I turned around. There stood a little, round, fat man with a brown face and white clothes, a first-class-looking little man, with a four-karat diamond on his finger and his eye full of interrogations and respects. I judged he was a kind of foreigner — may be from Russia or Japan or the archipelagoes.

"'Hist!' says the round man, full of concealments and confidences. ' Will the senor respect the discov-eryments he has made, that the mans on the ship shall not be acquaint ? The senor will be a gentle man that shall not expose one thing that by accident occur.'

" ' Monseer,' says I—for I judged him to be a kind of Frenchman —' receive my most exasperated assur ances that your secret is safe with James Clancy. Fur thermore, I will go so far as to remark, Veev la Lib erty — veev it good and strong. Whenever you hear of a Clancy obstructin' the abolishment of existin* governments you may notify me by return mail.'

"'The senor is good,' says the dark, fat man, smilin' under his black mustache. 'Wish yq|i to come aboard my ship and drink of wine a glass.'

" Bern' a Clancy, in two minutes me and the for eign man were seated at a table in the cabin of the steamer, with a bottle between us. I could hear the heavy boxes bein' dumped into the hold. I judged that cargo must consist of at least 2,000 Winchesters. Me and the brown man drank the bottle of stuff, and he called the steward to bring another. When you amalgamate a Clancy with the contents of a bottle you practically instigate secession. I had heard a good deal about these revolutions in them tropical localities, and I begun to want a hand in it.

"' You goin' to stir things up in your country, ain't you, monseer ?' says I, with a wink to let him know I was on.

"' Yes, yes,' said the little man, pounding his fist on the table. ' A change of the greatest will occur. Too long have the people been oppressed with the promises and the never-to-happen things to become. The great work it shall be carry on. Yes. Our forces shall in the capital city strike of the soonest. Carrambos!'

" * Carrambos is the word/ says I, beginning to in vest myself with enthusiasm and more wine,' likewise veeva, as I said before. May the shamrock of old — I mean the banana-vine or the pie-plant, or whatever the imperial emblem may be of your down-trodden country, wave forever.'

"'A thousand thank-yous,' says the round man, *for your emission of amicable utterances. What our cause needs of the very most is mans who will the work do, to lift it along. Oh, for one thousands strong, good mans to aid the General De Vega that he shall to his country bring those success and glory! It is hard — oh, so hard to find good mans to help in the work.'

"Monseer,' says I, leanin' over the table and graspin' his hand, * I don't know where your country is, but me heart bleeds for it. The heart of a Clancy was never deaf to the sight of an oppressed people. The family is filibusterers by birth, and foreigners by trade. If you can use James Clancy's arm and his blood in denudin' your shores of the tyrant's yoke they're yours to command.'

" General De Vega was overcome with joy to con-

fiscate my condolence of his conspiracies and predica ments. He tried to embrace me across the table, but his fatness, and the wine that had been in the bot tles, prevented. Thus was I welcomed into the ranks of filibustery. Then the general man told me his country had the name of Guatemala, and was the greatest nation laved by any ocean whatever any where. He looked at me with tears in his eyes, and from time to time he would emit the remark,' Ah! big, strong, brave mans! That is what my country need.'

" General De Vega, as was the name by which he denounced himself, brought out a documentor me to sign, which I did, makin' a fine flourish and curlycue with the tail of the'y'.

"'Your passage-money,' says the general, busi nesslike, 'shall from your pay be deduct.'

"' Twill not,' says I, haughty. ' I'll pay my own passage.' A hundred and eighty dollars I had in my inside pocket, and 'twas no common filibuster I was goin' to be, filibusterin' for me board and clothes

" The steamer was to sail in two hours, and I went ashore to get some things together I 'd need. When I came aboard I showed the general with pride the

The Shamrock and the Palm 185 outfit. 'Twas a fine Chinchilla overcoat, Arctic over shoes, fur cap and earmuffs, with elegant fleece-lined gloves and woolen muffler.

"' Carrambos ! ' says the little general. * What clothes are these that shall go to the tropic ?' And then the little spalpeen laughs, and he calls the captain, and the captain calls the purser, and they pipe up the chief engineer, and the whole gang leans against the cabin and laughs at Clancy's wardrobe for Guatemala.

" I reflects a bit, serious, and asks the general again to denominate the terms by which his countiy is called. He tells me, and I see then that 'twas the t'other one, Kamchatka, I had in mind. Since then I've had difficulty in separatin' the two nations in name, climate and geographic disposition.

"I paid my passage — twenty-four dollars, first cabin — and ate at table with the officer crowd. Down on the lower deck was a gang of second-class passengers, about forty of them, seemin' to be Da goes and the like. I wondered what so many of them were goin' along for.

" Well, then, in three days we sailed alongside that Guatemala. 'Twas a blue country, and not yellow,

as 'tis miscolored on the map. We landed at a town on the coast, where a train of cars was waitin' for us on a dinky little railroad. The boxes on the steamer were brought ashore and loaded on the cars. The gang of Dagoes got aboard, too, the general and me in the front car. Yes, me and General De Vega headed the revolution, as it pulled out of the seaport town. That train travelled about as fast as a policeman goin' to a riot. It penetrated the most conspicuous lot of fuzzy scenery ever seen outside a geography. We run some forty miles in seven hours, and the train stopped. There was no more railroad. 'Twas a sort of camp in a damp gorge full of wildness and melancholies. They was gradin' and choppin' out the forests ahead to continue the road. * Here,' says I to myself,' is the romantic haunt of the revolution ists. Here will Clancy, by the virtue that is in a superior race and the inculcation of Fenian tactics, strike a tremendous blow for liberty.'

" They unloaded the boxes from the train and be gun to knock the tops off. From the first one that was open I saw General De Vega take the Winchester rifles and pass them around to a squad of morbid sol-

The Shamrock and the Palm 187 diery. The other boxes was opened next, and, be lieve me or not, divil another gun was to be seen. Every other box in the load was full of pickaxes and spades.

" And then — sorrow be upon them tropics — the proud Clancy and the dishonoured Dagoes, each one of them, had to shoulder a pick or a spade, and march away to work on that dirty little railroad. Yes; 'twas that the Dagoes shipped for, and 'twas that the fili-busterin' Clancy signed for, though unbeknownst to himself at the time. In after days I found out about it. It seems 'twas hard to get hands to work on that road. The intelligent natives of the country was too lazy to work. Indeed, the saints know, 'twas unnec essary. By stretchin' out one hand, they could seize the most delicate and costly fruits of the earth, and, by stretchin' out the other, they could sleep for days at a time without hearin' a seven-o'clock whistle or the footsteps of the rent man upon the stairs. So, regular, the steamers travelled to the United States to seduce labour. Usually the imported spade-slingers died in two or three months from eatin' the over-ripe water and breathin' the violent tropical scenery.

Wherefore they made them sign contracts for a year, when they hired them, and put an armed guard over the poor divils to keep them from runnin' away.

' 'Twas thus I was double-crossed by the tropics through a family failin' of goin' out of the way to hunt disturbances.

" They gave me a pick, and I took it, meditatin* an insurrection on the spot; but there was the guards handlin' the Winchesters careless, and I come to the conclusion that discretion was the best part of filibus-terin'. There was about a hundred of us in the gang startin* out to work, and the word was given to move. I steps out of the ranks and goes up to that General De Vega man, who was smokin' a cigar and gazin* upon the scene with satisfactions and glory. He smiles at me polite and devilish. £ Plenty work/ says he, for big, strong mans in Guatemala. Yes. T'irty dollars in the month. Good pay. Ah, yes. You strong, brave man. Bimeby we push those railroad in the capital very quick. They want you go work now. Adios, strong mans.'

"'Monseer,' says I, lingerin', 'will you tell a poor little Irishman this: When I set foot on your cock-

The Shamrock and the Palm 189 roachy steamer, and breathed liberal and revolution ary sentiments into your sour wine, did you think I was conspirin' to sling a pick on your contemptuous little railroad ? And when you answered me with pat riotic recitations, humping up the star-spangled cause of liberty, did you have meditations of reducin' me to the ranks of the stump-grubbin' Dagoes in the chain-gangs of your vile and grovelin' country ?'

"The general man expanded his rotundity and laughed considerable. Yes, he laughed very long and loud, and I, Clancy, stood and waited.

"'Comical mans!' he shouts, at last. 'So you will kill me from the laughing. Yes; it is hard to find the brave, strong mans to aid my country. Rev olutions ? Did I speak of r-r-revolutions ? Not one word. I say, big, strong mans is need in Guatemala. So. The mistake is of you. You have looked in those one box containing those gun for the guard. You think all boxes is contain gun ? No.

"There is not war in Guatemala. But work? Yes. Good. T'irty dollar in the month. You shall shoulder one pickaxe, sefior, and dig for the liberty
        and prosperity of Guatemala. Off to your work.

The guard waits for you/

' * Little, fat, poodle dog of a brown man,' says I, quiet, but full of indignations and discomforts,' things shall happen to you. Maybe not right away, but as soon as J. Clancy can formulate somethin' in the way of repartee.'

" The boss of the gang orders us to work. I tramps off with the Dagoes, and I hears the distinguished patriot and kidnapper laughin' hearty as we go.

" 'Tis a sorrowful fact, for eight weeks I built rail roads for that misbehavin' country. I filibustered twelve hours a day with a heavy pick and a spade, choppin' away the luxurious landscape that grew up on the right of way. We worked in swamps that smelled like there was a leak in the gas mains, tramp-in' down a fine assortment of the most expensive hot house plants and vegetables. The scene was tropi cal beyond the wildest imagination of the geography man. The trees was all sky-scrapers; the under brush was full of needles and pins; there was mon keys jumpin' around and crocodiles and pink-tailed mockin'-birds, and ye stood knee-deep in the rotten

The Shamrock and the Palm 191 water and grabbled roots for the liberation of Guate mala. Of nights we would build smudges in camp to discourage the mosquitoes, and sit in the smoke, with the guards pacin' all around us. There was two hundred men workin' on the road — mostly Dagoes, nigger-men, Spanish-men and Swedes. Three or four were Irish.

" One old man named Halloran — a man of Hiber nian entitlements and discretions, explained it to me. He had been workin' on the road a year. Most of them died in less than six months. He was dried up to gristle and bone, and shook with chills every third night.

"'When you first come,' says he, ye think ye'll leave right away. But they hold out your first month's pay for your passage over, and by that time the tropics has its grip on ye. Ye're surrounded by a ragin' forest full of disreputable beasts — lions and baboons and anacondas — waitin' to devour ye. The sun strikes ye hard, and melts the marrow in your bones. Ye get similar to the lettuce-eaters the poetry-book speaks about. Ye forget the elevated sintiments of life, such as patriotism, revenge, dis-

turbances of the peace and the dacint love of a clane shirt. Ye do your work, and ye swallow the kerosene ile and rubber pipestems dished up to ye by the Dago cook for food. Ye light your pipeful, and say to yoursilf, " Nixt week I'll break away," and ye go to sleep and call yersilf a liar, for ye know ye'll never do it.'

" * Who is this general man,' asks I, * that calls him self De Vega?'

' 'Tis the man,' says Halloran, * who is tryin' to complete the finishin' of the railroad. 'Twas the proj ect of a private corporation, but it busted, and then the government took it up. De Vegy is a big poli tician, and wants to be prisident. The people want the railroad completed, as they're taxed mighty on account of it. The De Vegy man is pushin' it along as a campaign move.'

"Tis not my way,' says I, 'to make threats against any man, but there's an account to be settled between the railroad man and James O'Dowd Clancy.'

"' 'Twas that way I thought, mesilf, at first,' Hal loran says, with a big sigh,' until I got to be a lettuce-

The Shamrock and the Palm 193 eater. The fault's wid these tropics. They rejuices a man's system. 'Tis a land, as the poet says, "Where it always seems to be after dinner." I does me work and smokes me pipe and sleeps. There's little else in life, anyway. Ye'll get that way yersilf, mighty soon. Don't be harbourin' any sintiments at all, Clancy.'

"'I can't help it,' says I; 'I'm full of 'em. I en listed in the revolutionary army of this dark country in good faith to fight for its liberty, honours and silver candlesticks; instead of which I am set to amputatin* its scenery and grubbin' its roots. 'Tis the general man will have to pay for it.'

"Two months I worked on that railroad before I found a chance to get away. One day a gang of us was sent back to the end of the completed line to fetch some picks that had been sent down to Port Barrios to be sharpened. They were brought on a hand-car, and I noticed, when I started away, that the car was left there on the track.

" That night, about twelve, I woke up Halloran and told him my scheme.

"Run away?' says Halloran. 'Good Lord, Clancy, do ye mean it ? Why, I ain't got the nerve.

It's too chilly, and I ain't slept enough. Run away ? I told you, Clancy, I've eat the lettuce. I've lost my grip. 'Tis the tropics that's done it. 'Tis like the poet says: " Forgotten are our friends that we have left behind; in the hollow lettuce-land we will live and lay reclined." You better go on, Clancy. I'll stay, I guess. It's too early and cold, and I'm sleepy.' " So I had to leave Halloran. I dressed quiet, and slipped out of the tent we were in. When the guard came along I knocked him over, like a ninepin, with a green cocoanut I had, and made for the railroad. I got on that hand-car and made it fly. 'Twas yet a while before daybreak when I saw the lights of Port Barrios about a mile away. I stopped the hand-car there and walked to the town. I stepped inside the corporations of that town with care and hesitations. I was not afraid of the army of Guatemala, but me soul quaked at the prospect of a hand-to-hand struggle with its employment bureau. 'Tis a country that hires its help easy and keeps 'em long. Sure I can fancy Missis America and Missis Guatemala passin' a bit of gossip some fine, still night across the moun tains. 'Oh, dear,' says Missis America, 'and it's a

The Shamrock and the Palm 195 lot of trouble I'm havin' ag'in with the help, senora, ma'am.' 'Laws, now!' says Missis Guatemala, 'you dont' say so, ma'am! Now, mine never think of leav-in' me—te-he! ma'am/ snickers Missis Guatemala.

"I was wonderin' how I was goin' to move away from them tropics without bein' hired again. Dark as it was, I could see a steamer ridin' in the harbour, with smoke emergin' from her stacks. I turned down a little grass street that run down to the water. On the beach I found a little brown nigger-man just about to shove off in a skiff.

"' Hold on, Sambo/ says I,' sawe English ?'

"' Heap plenty, yes,' says he, with a pleasant grin.

"' What steamer is that ?' I asks him,' and where is it going ? And what's the news, and the good word and the time of day ?'

"'That steamer the Conchita,' said the brown man, affable and easy, rollin' a cigarette. 'Him come from New Orleans for load banana. Him got load last night. I think him sail in one, two hour. Verree nice day we shall be goin' have. You hear some talkee 'bout big battle, maybe so ? You think catchee General De Vega, sefior ? Yes ? No ?'

" (How's that, Sambo?' says I, 'Big battle? What battle ? Who wants catchee General De Vega ? I've been up at my gold mines in the interior for a couple of months, and haven't heard any news.'

"'Oh,' says the nigger-man, proud to speak the English, 'verree great revolution in Guatemala one week ago. General De Vega, him try be president. Him raise armee — one — five — ten thousand mans for fight at the government. Those one govern ment send five — forty — hundred thousand soldier to suppress revolution. They fight big battle yester day at Lomagrande — that about nineteen or fifty mile in the mountain. That government soldier wheep General De Vega — oh, most bad. Five hun dred — nine hundred — two thousand of his mans is kill. That revolution is smash suppress — bust — very quick. General De Vega, him r-r-run away fast on one big mule. Yes, carrambos ! The general, him r-r-run away, and his armee is kill. That gov ernment soldier, they try find General De Vega verree much. They want catchee him for shoot. You think they catchee that general, senor ?'

"' Saints grant it!' says I. ' 'Twould be the judg-

The Shamrock and the Palm 197 ment of Providence for settin' the warlike talent of a Clancy to gradin* the tropics with a pick and shovel. But 'tis not so much a question of insurrections now, me little man, as 'tis of the hired-man problem. 'Tis anxious I am to resign a situation of responsibility and trust with the white wings department of your great and degraded country. Row me in your little boat out to that steamer, and I'll give ye five dollars — sinker pacers — sinker pacers/ says I, reducin' the offer to the language and denomination of the tropic dialects.

" l Cinco pesos, 9 repeats the little man. ' Five dol-lee, you give ?'

" 'Twas not such a bad little man. He had hesita tions at first, sayin' that passengers leavin' the coun try had to have papers and passports, but at last he took me out alongside the steamer.

" Day was just breakin' as we struck her, and there wasn't a soul to be seen on board. The water was very still, and the nigger-man gave me a lift from the boat, and I climbed onto the steamer where her side was sliced to the deck for loadin' fruit. The hatches was open, and I looked down and saw the cargo of

bananas that filled the hold to within six feet of
the top. I thinks to myself, 'Clancy, you better
go as a stowaway. It's safer. The steamer men
might hand you back to the employment bureau.
The tropics'll get you, Clancy, if you don't watch
out.'

"So I jumps down easy among the bananas, and digs out a hole to hide in among the bunches. In an hour or so I could hear the engines goin', and feel the steamer rockin', and I knew we were off to sea. They left the hatches open for ventilation, and pretty soon it was light enough in the hold to see fairly well. I got to feelin' a bit hungry, and thought I'd have a light fruit lunch, by way of refreshment. I creeped out of the hole I'd made and stood up straight. Just then I saw another man crawl up about ten feet away and reach out and skin a banana and stuff it into his mouth. 'Twas a dirty man, black-faced and ragged and disgraceful of aspect. Yes, the man was a ringer for the pictures of the fat Weary Willie in the funny papers. I looked again, and saw it was my general man — De Vega, the great revolutionist, mule-rider and pick-axe importer. When he saw me the general

The Shamrock and the Palm 199 hesitated with his mouth filled with banana and his eyes the size of cocoanuts.

"' Hist!' I says. ' Not a word, or they'll put us off and make us walk. " Veev la Liberty!" ' I adds, copperin' the sentiment by shovin' a banana into the source of it. I was certain the general wouldn't rec ognize me. The nefarious work of the tropics had left me lookin' different. There was half an inch of roan whiskers coverin' me face, and me costume was a pair of blue overalls and a red shirt.

" How you come in the ship, senor ?' asked the general as soon as he could speak.

"'By the back door —whist!' says I. "Twas a glorious blow for liberty we struck,' I continues: * but we was overpowered by numbers. Let us accept our defeat like brave men and eat another banana.'

: ' Were you in the cause of liberty fightin', senor ? ' says the general, sheddin' tears on the cargo.

"' To the last,' says I. ' 'Twas I led the last des perate charge against the minions of the tyrant. But it made them mad, and we was forced to retreat. 'Twas I, general, procured the mule upon which you escaped. Could you give that ripe bunch a little

boost this way, general ? It's a bit out of my reach.

Thanks.'

"'Say you so, brave patriot?' said the general, again weepin'. 'Ah, Dios! And I have not the means to reward your devotion. Barely did I my life bring away. Carrambos ! what a devil's animal was that mule, senor! Like ships in one storm was I dashed about. The skin on myself was ripped away with the thorns and vines. Upon the bark of a hun dred trees did that beast of the infernal bump, and cause outrage to the legs of mine. In the night to Port Barrios I came. I dispossess myself of that mountain of mule and hasten along the water shore. I find a little boat to be tied. I launch myself and row to the steamer. I cannot see any mans on board, so I climbed one rope which hang at the side. I then myself hide in the bananas. Surely, I say, if the ship captains view me, they shall throw me again to those Guatemala. Those things are not good. Guate mala will shoot General De Vega. Therefore, I am hide and remain silent. Life itself is glorious. Lib erty, it is pretty good; but so good as life I do not think.'

The Shamrock and the Palm 201 " Three days, as I said, was the trip to New Orleans. The general man and me got to be cronies of the deep est dye. Bananas we ate until they were distasteful to the sight and an eyesore to the palate, but to ba nanas alone was the bill of fare reduced. At night I crawls out, careful, on the lower deck, and gets a bucket of fresh water.

" That General De Vega was a man inhabited by an engorgement of words and sentences. He added to the monotony of the voyage by divestin' himself of conversation. He believed I was a revolutionist of his own party, there bein', as he told me, a good many Americans and other foreigners in its ranks. 'Twas a braggart and a conceited little gabbler it was, though he considered himself a hero. 'Twas on him self he wasted all his regrets at the failin* of his plot. Not a word did the little balloon have to say about the other misbehavin' idiots that had been shot, or run themselves to death in his revolution.

" The second day out he was feelin' pretty braggy and uppish for a stowed-away conspirator that owed his existence to a mule and stolen bananas. He was tellin' me about the great railroad he had been build-

Cabbages and Kings in', and he relates what he calls a comic incident about a fool Irishman he inveigled from New Orleans to sling a pick on his little morgue of a narrow-gauge line. 'Twas sorrowful to hear the little, dirty general tell the opprobrious story of how he put salt upon the tail of that reckless and silly bird, Clancy. Laugh, he did, hearty and long. He shook with laughin', the black-faced rebel and outcast, standin' neck-deep in bananas, without friends or country.

" f Ah, senor/ he snickers,' to the death you would have laughed at that drollest Irish. I say to him: " Strong, big mans is need very much in Guatemala." " I will blows strike for your down-pressed country," he say. " That shall you do," I teU him. Ah! it was an Irish so comic. He sees one box break upon the wharf that contain for the guard a few gun. He think there is gun in all the box. But that is all pick-axe. Yes. Ah! senor, could you the face of that Irish have seen when they set him to the work!'

" 'Twas thus the ex-boss of the employment bureau contributed to the tedium of the trip

with merry jests and anecdote. But now and then he would weep

The Shamrock and the Palm 203 upon the bananas and make oration about the lost cause of liberty and the mule.

" 'Twas a pleasant sound when the steamer bump ed against the pier in New Orleans. Pretty soon we heard the pat-a-pat of hundreds of bare feet, and the Dago gang that unloads the fruit jumped on the deck and down into the hold. Me and the general worked a while at passin' up the bunches, and they thought we were part of the gang. After about an hour we managed to slip off the steamer onto the wharf.

" 'Twas a great honour on the hands of an obscure Clancy, havin' the entertainment of the representa tive of a great foreign filibuster-in' power. I first bought for the general and myself many long drinks and things to eat that were not bananas. The gen eral man trotted along at my side, leavin' all the ar rangements to me. I led him up to Lafayette Square and set him on a bench in the little park. Cigarettes I had bought for him, and he humped himself down on the seat like a little, fat, contented hobo. I look him over as he sets there, and what I see pleases me. Brown by nature and instinct, he is now brindled with dirt and dust. Praise to the mule, his clothes

r

204 Cabbages and Kings

is mostly strings and flaps. Yes, the looks of the

general man is agreeable to Clancy.

" I asks him, delicate, if, by any chance, he brought away anybody's money with him from Guatemala. He sighs and humps his shoulders against the bench. Not a cent. All right. Maybe, he tells me, some of his friends in the tropic outfit will send him funds later. The general was as clear a case of no visible means as I ever saw.

" I told him not to move from the bench, and then I went up to the comer of Poydras and Carondelet. Along there is O'Hara's beat. In five minutes along comes O'Hara, a big, fine man, red-faced, with shinin' buttons, swingin' his club. 'Twould be a fine thing for Guatemala to move into O'Hara's precinct. 'Twould be a fine bit of recreation for Danny to sup press revolutions and uprisin's once or twice a week with his club.

"' Is 5046 workin' yet, Danny ?' says I, walkin' up to him.

"' Overtime/ says O'Hara, lookin* over me sus picious. ' Want some of it ? '

" Fifty-forty-six is the celebrated city ordinance au^

The Shamrock and the Palm 205 thorizin' arrest, conviction and imprisonment of per sons that succeed in eoncealin' their crimes from the police.

t(< Don't ye know Jimmy Clancy?' says I. 'Ye pink-gilled monster.' So, when O'Hara recognized me beneath the scandalous exterior bestowed upon me by the tropics, I backed him into a doorway and told him what I wanted, and why I wanted it. * All right, Jimmy,' says O'Hara. ' Go back and hold the bench. I'll be along in ten minutes.'

" In that time O'Hara strolled through Lafayette Square and spied two Weary Willies disgracin' one of the benches. In ten minutes more J. Clancy and General De Vega, late candidate for the presidency of Guatemala, was in the station house. The general is badly frightened, and calls upon me to proclaim his distinguishments and rank.

"' The man,' says I to the police,' used to be a rail road man. He's on the bum now. 'Tis a little bug house he is, on account of losin' his job.'

" 'Carrambos I' says the general, fizzin' like a little soda-water fountain, 'you fought, sefior, with my forces in my native country. Why do you say the

206 Cabbages and Kings

lies ? You shall say I am the General De Vega, one
soldier, one cabattero —'

" ' Railroader,' says I again. ' On the hog. No good. Been livin' for three days on stolen bananas. Look at him. Ain't that enough ?'

"Twenty-five dollars or sixty days, was what the recorder gave the general. He didn't have a cent, so he took the time. They let me go, as I knew they would, for I had money to show, and O'Hara spoke for me. Yes; sixty days he got. 'Twas just so long that I slung a pick for the great country of Kam — Guatemala."

Clancy paused. The bright starlight showed a reminiscent look of happy content on his seasoned features. Keogh leaned in his chair and gave his partner a slap on his thinly-clad back that sounded like the crack of the surf on the sands.

" Tell 'em, ye divil," he chuckled, " how you got even with the tropical general in the way of agricul tural manceuvrings."

" Havin* no money," concluded Clancy, with unc tion, " they set him to work his fine out with a gang from the parish prison clearing Ursulines Street

The Shamrock and the Palm 207 Around the corner was a saloon decorated genially with electric fans and cool merchandise. I made that me headquarters, and every fifteen minutes I'd walk around and take a look at the little man filibus-terin' with a rake and shovel. 'Twas just such a hot broth of a day as this has been. And I'd call at him ' Hey, monseer!* and he'd look at me black, with the damp showin' through his shirt in places.

"' Fat, strong mans/ says I to General De Vega, * is needed in New Orleans. Yes. To carry on the good work. Carrambos! Erin go bragh!' "

CHAPTER ELEVEN

The Remnants of the Code

BREAKFAST in Coralio was at eleven. There fore the people did not go to market early. The little wooden market-house stood on a patch of short-trimmed grass, under the vivid green foliage of a bread-fruit tree.

Thither one morning the venders leisurely con vened, bringing their wares with them. A porch or platform six feet wide encircled the building, shaded from the mid-morning sun by the projecting, grass-thatched roof. Upon this platform the venders were wont to display their goods — newly-killed beef, fish, crabs, fruit of the country, cassava, eggs, dulces and high, tottering stacks of native tortillas as large around as the sombrero of a Spanish grandee.

The Remnants of the Code 209 But on this morning they whose stations lay on the seaward side of the market-house, instead of spread ing their merchandise formed themselves into a softly jabbering and gesticulating group. For there upon their space of the platform was sprawled, asleep, the unbeautiful figure of " Beelzebub " Blythe. He lay upon a ragged strip of cocoa matting, more than ever a fallen angel in appearance. His suit of coarse flax, soiled, bursting at the seams, crumpled into a thou sand diversified wrinkles and creases, inclosed him absurdly, like the garb of some effigy that had been stuffed in sport and thrown there after indignity had been wrought upon it. But firmly upon the high bridge of his nose reposed his gold-rimmed glasses, the surviving badge of his ancient glory.

The sun's rays, reflecting quiveringly from the rip pling sea upon his face, and the voices of the market-men woke " Beelzebub " Blythe. He sat up, blink ing, and leaned his back against the wall of the mar ket. Drawing a blighted silk handkerchief from his pocket, he assiduously rubbed and burnished his glasses. And while doing this he became aware that his bedroom had been invaded, and that polite brown and yellow men were beseeching him to vacate in fa vour of their market stuff.

If the senor would have the goodness — a thousand pardons for bringing to him molestation —- but soon would come the compradores for the day's provisions — surely they had ten thousand regrets at disturbing him!

In this manner they expanded to him the intima tion that he must clear out and cease to clog the wheels of trade.

Blythe stepped from the platform with the air of a prince leaving his canopied couch. He never quite lost that air, even at the lowest point of his fall. It is clear that the college of good breeding does not necessarily maintain a chair of morals within its walls.

Blythe shook out his wry clothing, and moved slowly up the Calle Grande through the hot sand. He moved without a destination in his mind. The Kttle town was languidly stirring to its daily life. Golden-skinned babies tumbled over one another in the grass. The sea breeze brought him appetite, but nothing to satisfy it. Throughout Coralio were its morning odors — those from the heavily \'7bragrant

The Remnants of the Code 211 tropical flowers and from the bread baking in the outdoor ovens of clay and the pervading smoke of their fires. Where the smoke cleared, the crystal air, with some of the efficacy of faith, seemed to remove the mountains almost to the sea, bringing them so near that one might count the scarrecj glades

1p»-«*

on their wooded sides. The light-footed Caribs were swiftly gliding to their tasks at the waterside. Al ready along the bosky trails from the banana groves files of horses were slowly moving, concealed, except for their nodding heads and plodding'legs, by the bunches of green-golden fruit heaped upon their backs. On doorsills sat women combing their long, black hair and calling, one to another, across the nar row thoroughfares. Peace reigned in Coralio — arid and bald peace; but still peace.

On that bright morning when Nature seemed to be offering the lotus onfce Dawn's golden platter " Beekebul?" Blythe had Cached rock bottom. Fur ther descent seemed impossible. That last night's slumber in a public place had done for him. As long as he had had a roof to cover him there had remained, unbridged, the space that separates a gentleman

Cabbages and Kings from the beasts of the jungle and the fowls of the air. But now he was little more than a whimpering oyster led to be devoured on the sands of a Southern sea by the artful walrus, Circumstance, and the impla cable carpenter, Fate.

To Blythe money was now but a memory. He had drained his friends of all that their good-fellow ship had to offer; then he had squeezed them to the last drop of their generosity; and at the last, Aaron-like, he had smitten the rock of their hardening bosoms for the scattering, ignoble drops of Charity itself.

He had exhausted his credit to the last reed. With the minute keenness of the shameless sponger he was aware of every source in Coralio from which a glass of rum, a meal or a piece of silver could be wheedled. Marshalling each such source in his mind, he con sidered it with all the thoroughness and penetration that hunger and thirst lent him for the task. All his optimism failed to thresh a grain of hope from the chaff of his postulations. He had played out the game. That one night in the open had shaken his nerves. Until then there had been left to him at

The Remnants of the Code 213 least a few grounds upon which he could base his unblushing demands upon his neighbours' stores. Now he must beg instead of borrowing. The most brazen sophistry could not dignify by the name of " loan " the coin contemptuously flung to a beach comber who slept on the bare boards of the public market.

But on this morning no beggar would have more thankfully received a charitable coin, for the demon thirst had him by the throat — the drunkard's matutinal thirst that requires to be slaked at each morning station on the road to Tophet

Blythe walked slowly up the street, keeping a watchful eye for any miracle that might drop manna upon him in his wilderness. As he passed the popular eating house of Madama Vasquez, Madama's boarders were just sitting down to freshly-baked bread, aguacates, pines and delicious coffee that sent forth odorous guarantee of its quality upon the breeze. Madama was serving; she turned her shy, stolid, melancholy gaze for a moment out the window; she saw Blythe, and her expression turned more shy and embarrassed. " Beelzebub " owed her twenty pesos.

He bowed as he had once bowed to less embarrassed dames to whom he owed nothing, and passed on.

Merchants and their clerks were throwing open the solid wooden doors of their shops. Polite but cool were the glances they cast upon Blythe as he lounged tentatively by with the remains of his old jaunty air; for they were his creditors almost without exception.

At the little fountain in the plaza he made an apology for a toilet with his wetted handkerchief. Across the open square filed the dolorous line of friends to the prisoners in the calaboza, bearing the morning meal of the immured. The food in their hands aroused small longing in Blythe. It was drink that his soul craved, or money to buy it.

In the streets he met many with whom he had been friends and equals, and whose patience and liberality he had gradually exhausted. Willard Geddie and Paula cantered past him with the coolest of nods, returning from their daily horseback ride along the old Indian road. Keogh passed him at another corner, whistling cheerfully and bearing a prize of newly-laid eggs for the breakfast of himself and Clancy.

The Remnants of the Code 215 The jovial scout of Fortune was one of Blythe's victims who had plunged his hand oftenest into his pocket to aid him. But now it seemed that Keogh, too, had fortified himself against further invasions. His curt greeting and the ominous light in his full, grey eye quickened the steps of " Beelzebub," whom desperation had almost incited to attempt an additional "loan."

  *

Three drinking shops the forlorn one next visited in succession. In all of these his money, his credit and his welcome had long since been spent; but Blythe felt that he would have fawned in the dust at the feet of an enemy that morning for one draught of aguardiente. In two of the pulperias his courageous petition for drink was met with a refusal so polite that it stung worse than abuse. The third establishment had acquired something of American methods; and here he was seized bodily and cast out upon his hands and knees.

This physical indignity caused a singular change in the man. As he picked himself up and walked away, an expression of absolute relief came upon his features. The specious and conciliatory smile that had been graven there was succeeded by a look of calm and sinister resolve. "Beelzebub" had been floundering in the sea of improbity, holding by a slender life-line to the respectable world that had cast him overboard. He must have felt that with this ultimate shock the line had snapped, and have experienced the welcome ease of the drowning swimmer who has ceased to struggle.

Blythe walked to the next corner and stood there while he brushed the sand from his garments and re-polished his glasses.

"I've got to do it — oh, I've got to do it," he told himself, aloud. " If I had a quart of rum I believe I could stave it off yet — for a little while. But there's no more rum for — * Beelzebub,' as they call me. By the flames of Tartarus! if I'm to sit at the right hand of Satan somebody has got to pay the court expenses. You'll have to pony up, Mr. Frank Goodwin. You're a good fellow; but a gentleman must draw the line at being kicked into the gutter. Blackmail isn't a pretty word, but it's the next station on the road I'm travelling."

With purpose in his steps Blythe now moved

The Remnants of ilw Code 217 rapidly through the town by way of its landward environs. He passed through the squalid quarters of the improvident negroes and on beyond the pic turesque shacks of the poorer mestizos. From many points along his course he could see, through the umbrageous glades, the house of Frank Goodwin on its wooded hill. And as he crossed the little bridge over the lagoon he saw the old Indian, Galvez, scrub bing at the wooden slab that bore the name of Mira-flores. Beyond the lagoon the lands of Goodwin began to slope gently upward. A grassy road, shaded by a munificent and diverse array of tropical flora wound from the edge of an outlying banana grove to the dwelling. Blythe took this road with long and purposeful strides.

Goodwin was seated on his coolest gallery, dictat ing letters to his secretary, a sallow and capable native youth. The household adhered to the Ameri can plan of breakfast; and that meal had been a thing of the past for the better part of an hour.

The castaway walked to the steps, and flourished a hand.

"Good morning, Blythe," said Goodwin, looking

Cabbages and Kings

up. " Come in and have a chair. Anything I can do for you ? "

" I want to speak to you in private."

Goodwin nodded at his secretary, who strolled out under a mango tree and lit a cigarette. Blythe took the chair that he had left vacant.

" I want some money," he began, doggedly.

" I'm sorry," said Goodwin, with equal directness, " but you can't have any. You're drinking yourself to death, Blythe. Your friends have done all they could to help you to brace up. You won't help yourself. There's no use furnishing you with money to ruin yourself with any longer."

"Dear man/' said Blythe, tilting back his chair, "it isn't a question of social economy now. It's past that. I like you, Goodwin; and I've come to stick a knife between your ribs. I was kicked out of Espada's saloon this morning; and Society owes me reparation for my wounded feelings."

" I didn't kick you out."

"No; but in a general way you represent Society; and in a particular way you represent my last chance. I've had to come down to it, old man — I tried to do

The Remnants of the Code 219 it a month ago when Losada's man was here turning things over; but I couldn't do it then. Now it's different. I want a thousand dollars, Goodwin; and you'll have to give it to me."

" Only last week," said Goodwin, with a smile, " a silver dollar was all you were asking for."

" An evidence," said Blythe, flippantly, " that I was still virtuous — though under heavy pressure. The wages of sin should be something higher than a peso worth forty-eight cents. Let's talk business. I am the villain in the third act; and I must have my mer ited, if only temporary, triumph. I saw you collar the late president's valiseful of boodle. Oh, I know it's blackmail; but

I'm liberal about the price. I know I'm a cheap villain — one of the regular saw mill-drama kind — but you're one of my particular friends, and I don't want to stick you hard."

" Suppose you go into the details," suggested Good win, calmly arranging his letters on the table.

"All right," said "Beelzebub." "I like the way you take it. I despise histrionics; so you will please prepare yourself for the facts without any red fire, calcium or grace notes on the saxophone.

"On the night that His Fly-by-night Excellency arrived in town I was very drunk. You will excuse the pride with which I state that fact; but it was quite a feat for me to attain that desirable state. Some body had left a cot out under the orange trees in the yard of Madama Ortiz's hotel. I stepped over the wall, laid down upon it, and fell asleep. I was awakened by an orange that dropped from the tree upon my nose; and I laid there for awhile cursing Sir Isaac Newton, or whoever it was that invented gravi tation, for not confining his theory to apples.

" And then along came Mr. Miraflores and his true-love with the treasury in a valise, and went into the hotel. Next you hove in sight, and held a pow-wow with the tonsorial artist who insisted upon talking shop after hours. I tried to slumber again; but once more my rest was disturbed — this time by the noise of the popgun that went off upstairs. Then that valise came crashing down into an orange tree just above my head; and I arose from my couch, not knowing when it might begin to rain Saratoga trunks. When the army and the constabulary began to arrive, with their medals and decorations hastily pinned

The Remnants of the Code to their pajamas, and their snickersnees drawn, I crawled into the welcome shadow of a banana plant. I remained there for an hour, by which time the ex citement and the people had cleared away. And then, my dear Goodwin — excuse me — I saw you sneak back and pluck that ripe and juicy valise from the orange tree. I followed you, and saw you take it to your own house. A hundred-thousand-dollar crop from one orange tree in a season about breaks the record of the fruit-growing industry.

" Being a gentleman at that time, of course I never mentioned the incident to anyone. But this morn ing I was kicked out of a saloon, my code of honour is all out at the elbows, and I'd sell my mother's prayer-book for three fingers of aguardiente. I'm not putting on the screws hard. It ought to be worth a thousand to you for me to have slept on that cot through the whole business without waking up and seeing anything."

Goodwin opened two more letters, and made mem oranda in pencil on them. Then he called "Man uel !" to his secretary, who came, spryly.

" The Ariel— when does she sail ? " asked Goodwin.

" Sefior," answered the youth, " at three this after noon. She drops down-coast to Punta Soledad to complete her cargo of fruit. From there she sails for New Orleans without delay."

"Bueno!" said Goodwin. "These letters may wait yet awhile."

The secretary returned to his cigarette under the mango tree.

" In round numbers," said Goodwin, facing Blythe squarely, "how much money do you owe in this town, not including the sums you have 'borrowed* from me ? "

" Five hundred — at a rough guess," answered Blythe, lightly.

" Go somewhere in the town and draw up a sched ule of your debts," said Goodwin. " Come back here in two hours, and I will send Manuel with the money to pay them. I will also have a decent outfit of cloth ing ready for you. You will sail on the Ariel at three. Manuel will accompany you as far as the deck of the steamer. There he will hand you one thousand dollars in cash. I suppose that we needn't discuss what you will be expected to do in return."

The Remnants of the Code

* Oh, I understand," piped Blythe, cheerily. " I was asleep all the time on the cot under Madama Ortiz's orange trees; and I shake off the dust of Co-ralio forever. I'll play fair. No more of the lotus for me. Your proposition is O. K. You're a good fellow, Goodwin; and I let you off light. I'll agree to everything. But in the meantime — I've a devil of a thirst on, old man — "

" Not a centavo" said Goodwin, firmly, " until you are on board the Ariel. You would be drunk in thirty minutes if you had money now."

But he noticed the blood-streaked eyeballs, the re laxed form and the shaking hands of " Beelzebub;" and he stepped into the dining room through the low window, and brought out a glass and a decanter of brandy.

" Take a bracer, anyway, before you go," he pro posed, even as a man to the friend whom he enter-tarns.

" Beelzebub " Blythe's eyes glistened at the sight of the solace for which his soul burned. To-day for the first time his poisoned nerves had been denied their steadying dose; and their retort was a mounting

Cabbages and Kings torment. He grasped the decanter and rattled its crystal mouth against the glass in his trembling hand. He flushed the glass, and then stood erect, holding it aloft for an instant. For one fleeting mo ment he held his head above the drowning waves of his abyss. He nodded easily at Goodwin, raised his brimming glass and murmured a "health" that men had used in his ancient Paradise Lost. And then so suddenly that he spilled the brandy over his hand, he set down his glass, untasted.

" In two hours," his dry lips muttered to Goodwin, as he marched down the steps and turned his face toward the town.

In the edge of the cool banana grove "Beelzebub" halted, and snapped the tongue of his belt buckle into another hole.

" I couldn't do it," he explained, feverishly, to the waving banana fronds. " I wanted to, but I couldn't. A gentleman can't drink with the man that he black mails."

CHAPTER TWELVE

Shoes

JOHN DE GRAFFENREID ATWOOD ate of

the lotus, root, stem, and flower. The tropics gob bled him up. He plunged enthusiastically into his work, which was to try to forget Rosine.

Now, they who dine on the lotus rarely consume it plain. There is a sauce au diable that goes with it; and the distillers are the chefs who prepare it. And on Johnny's menu card it read " brandy." With a bottle between them, he and Billy Keogh would sit on the porch of the little consulate at night and roar out great, indecorous songs, until the natives, slipping hastily past, would shrug a shoulder and mutter things to themselves about the ec Americanos diablos"

One day Johnny's mozo brought the mail and

dumped it on the table. Johnny leaned from his hammock, and fingered the four or five letters de jectedly. Keogh was sitting on the edge of the table chopping lazily with a paper knife at the legs of a centipede that was crawling among the stationery. Johnny was in that phase of lotus-eating when all the world tastes bitter in one's mouth.

"Same old thing!" he complained. " Fool people writing for information about the country. They want to know all about raising fruit, and how to make a fortune without work. Half of 'em don't even send stamps for a reply. They think a consul hasn't anything to do but write letters. Slit those envelopes for me, old man, and see what they want. I'm feeling too rocky to move."

Keogh, acclimated beyond all possibility of ill-humour, drew his chair to the table with smiling com pliance on his rose-pink countenance, and began to slit open the letters. Four of them were from citi zens in various parts of the United States who seemed to regard the consul at Coralio as a cyclopaedia of information. They asked long lists of questions, numerically arranged, about the climate, products,

possibilities, laws, business chances, and statistics of the country in which the consul had the honour of representing his own government.

"Write 'em, please, Billy," said that inert official, "just a line, referring them to the latest consular report. Tell 'em the State Department will be de lighted to furnish the literary gems. Sign my name. Don't let your pen scratch, Billy; it'll keep me awake."

"Don't snore," said Keogh, amiably, "and I'll do your work for you. You need a corps of assist ants, anyhow. Don't see how you ever get out a report. Wake up a minute! — here's one more letter — it's from your own town, too — Dalesburg."

" That so ? " murmured Johnny showing a mild and obligatory interest. " What's it about ? "

" Postmaster writes," explained Keogh. " Says a citizen of the town wants some facts and advice from you. Says the citizen has an idea in his head of coming down where you are and opening a shoe store. Wants to know if you think the business would pay. Says he's heard of the boom along this coast, and wants to get in on the ground floor."

Cabbages and Kings

In spite of the heat and his bad temper, Johnny's hammock swayed with his laughter. Keogh laughed too; and the pet monkey on the top shelf of the book case chattered in shrill sympathy with the ironical reception of the letter from Dalesburg.

" Great bunions!" exclaimed the consul. " Shoe store! What'll they ask about next, I wonder? Overcoat factory, I reckon. Say, Billy — of our 3,000 citizens, how many do you suppose ever had on a pair of shoes ? "

Keogh reflected judicially.

" Let's see — there's you and me and —"

" Not me," said Johnny, promptly and incorrectly, holding up a foot encased in a disreputable deerskin zapato. "I haven't been a victim to shoes in months."

J'But you've got 'em, though," went on Keogh. "And there's Goodwin and Blanchard and Geddie and old Lutz and Doc Gregg and that Italian that's agent for the banana company, and there's old Delgado — no; he wears sandals. And, oh, yes; there's Madama Ortiz,' what kapes the hotel' — she had on a pair of red kid slippers at the baile the other

night. And Miss Pasa, her daughter, that went to school in the States — she brought back some civilized notions in the way of footgear. And there's the comandante's sister that dresses up her feet on feast-days — and Mrs. Geddie, who wears a two with a Castilian instep — and that's about all the ladies. Let's see — don't some of the soldiers at the cuartel — no: that's so; they're allowed shoes only when on the march. In barracks they turn their little toeses out to grass."

"'Bout right," agreed the consul. "Not over twenty out of the three thousand ever felt leather on their walking arrangements. Oh, yes; Coralio is just the town for an enterprising shoe store — that doesn't want to part with its goods. Wonder if old Patterson is trying to jolly me! He always was full of things he called jokes. Write him a letter, Billy. I'll dictate it. We'll jolly him back a few."

Keogh dipped his pen, and wrote at Johnny's dic tation. With many pauses, filled in with smoke and sundry travellings of the bottle and glasses, the fol lowing reply to the Dalesburg communication was perpetrated:

Mr. OBADIAH PATTEBSON, Dalesburg, Ala.

Dear Sir: In reply to your favour of July 2d, I have the honour to inform you that, according to my opinion, there is no place on the habitable globe that presents to the eye stronger evidence of the need of a first-class shoe store than does the town of Coralio. There are 3,000 inhabitants in -the place, and not a single shoe store! The situation speaks for itself. This coast is rapidly becoming the goal of enterpris ing business men, but the shoe business is one that has been sadly overlooked or neglected. In fact, there are a considerable number of our citizens ac tually without shoes at present.

Besides the want above mentioned, there is also a crying need for a brewery, a college of higher mathe matics, a coal yard, and a clean and intellectual Punch and Judy show. I have the honour to be, sir,

Your Obt. Servant, JOHN DE GRAFFENREID ATWOOD,

U. S. Consul at Cvralio.

P. S.-—Hello! Uncle Obadiah. How's the old burg racking along? What would the government do without you and me ? Look out for a green-headed parrot and a bunch of bananas soon, from your old friend JOHNNY.

" I throw in that postscript," explained the consul, " so Uncle Obadiah won't take offence at the official tone of the letter! Now, Billy, you get that corre spondence fixed up, and send Pancho to the post-office with it. The Ariadne takes the mail out to-morrow if they make up that load of fruit to-day."

The night programme in Coralio never varied. The recreations of the people were soporific and flat They wandered about, barefoot and aimless, speak ing lowly and smoking cigar or cigarette. Looking down on the dimly lighted ways one seemed to see a threading maze of brunette ghosts tangled with a procession of insane fireflies. In some houses the thrumming of lugubrious guitars added to the de pression of the triste night. Giant tree-frogs rattled in the foliage as loudly as the end man's " bones " in a minstrel troupe. By nine o'clock the streets were almost deserted.

Nor at the consulate was there often a change of bill. Keogh would come there nightly, for Coralio's one cool place was the little seaward porch of that official residence.

The brandy would be kept moving; and before

midnight sentiment would begin to stir in the heart of the self-exiled consul. Then he would relate to Keogh the story of his ended romance. Each night Keogh would listen patiently to the tale, and be ready with untiring sympathy.

"But don't you think for a minute" — thus Johnny would always conclude his woeful narrative — " that" I'm grieving about that girl, Billy. I've forgotten her. She never enters my mind. If she were to enter that door right now, my pulse wouldn't gain a beat. That's all over long ago."

"Don't I know it?" Keogh would answer. "Of course you've forgotten her. Proper thing to do. Wasn't quite O. K. of her to listen to the knocks that — er — Dink Pawson kept giving you."

"Pink Dawson!"—a world of contempt would be in Johnny's tones—"Poor white trash! That's what he was. Had five hundred acres of farming land, though; and that counted. Maybe I'll have a chance to get back at him some day. The Daw-sons weren't anybody. Everybody in Alabama knows the Atwoods. Say, Billy —did you know my mother was a De Graffenreid ? "

" Why, no," Keogh would say; " is that so ?" He had heard it some three hundred times.

" Fact. The De Graffenreids of Hancock County. But I never think of that girl any more, do I, Billy ? "

"Not for a minute, my boy," would be the last sounds heard by the conqueror of Cupid.

At this point Johnny would fall into a gentle slum ber, and Keogh would saunter out to his own shack under the calabash tree at the edge of the plaza.

In a day or two the letter from the Dalesburg post master and its answer had been forgotten by the Coralio exiles. But on the 26th day of July the fruit of the reply appeared upon the tree of events.

The Andador, a fruit steamer that visited Coralio regularly, drew into the offing and anchored. The beach was lined with spectators while the quarantine doctor and the custom-house crew rowed out to attend to their duties.

An hour later Billy Keogh lounged into the con sulate, clean and cool in his linen clothes, and grin ning like a pleased shark.

" Guess what ? " he said to Johnny, lounging in his hammock.

" Too hot to guess," said Johnny, lazily.

"Your shoe-store man's come," said Keogh, roll ing the sweet morsel on his tongue, " with a stock of goods big enough to supply the continent as far down as Terra del Fuego. They're carting his cases over to the custom-house now. Six barges full they brought ashore and have paddled back for the rest. Oh, ye saints in glory! won't there be regalements in the air when he gets onto the joke and has an inter view with Mr. Consul ? It'll be worth nine years in the tropics just to witness that one joyful moment."

Keogh loved to take his mirth easily. He selected a clean place on the matting and lay upon the floor. The walls shook with his enjoyment. Johnny turned half over and blinked.

"Don't tell me," he said, "that anybody was fool enough to take that letter seriously."

"Four-thousand-dollar stock of goods!" gasped Keogh, in ecstasy. " Talk about coals to Newcastle! Why didn't he take a ship-load of palm-leaf fans to Spitzbergen while he was about it? Saw the old codger on the beach. You ought to have been there when he put on his specs and squinted at the

five hundred or so barefooted citizens standing around."

" Are you telling the truth, Billy ?" asked the con sul, weakly.

" Am I ? You ought to see the buncoed gentleman's daughter he brought along. Looks! She makes the brick-dust senoritas here look like tar-babies."

"Go on," said Johnny, "if you can stop that asinine giggling. I hate to see a grown man make a laughing hyena of himself."

"Name is Hemstetter," went on Keogh. "He's a — Hello! what's the matter now ? "

Johnny's moccasined feet struck the floor with a thud as he wriggled out of his hammock.

"Get up, you idiot," he said, sternly, "or I'll brain you with this inkstand. That's Rosine and her father. Gad! what a drivelling idiot old Patter son is! Get up, here, Billy Keogh, and help me. What the devil are we going to do? Has all the world gone crazy ? "

Keogh rose and dusted himself. He managed to regain a decorous demeanour.

"Situation has got to be met, Johnny," he said, with some success at seriousness. " I didn't think about its being your girl until you spoke. First thing to do is to get them comfortable quarters. You go down and face the music, and I'll trot out to Good win's and see if Mrs. Goodwin won't take them in. They've got the decentest house in town."

"Bless you, Billy!" said the consul. "I knew you wouldn't desert me. The world's bound to come to an end, but maybe we can stave it off for a day or two."

Keogh hoisted his umbrella and set out for Good win's house. Johnny put on his coat and hat. He picked up the brandy bottle, but set it down-again without drinking, and marched bravely down to the beach.

In the shade of the custom-house walls he found Mr. Hemstetter and Rosine surrounded by a mass of gaping citizens. (The customs officers were duck ing and scraping, while the captain of the Andador interpreted the business of the new arrivals/ Rosine looked healthy and very much alive. She was gazing at the strange scenes around her with amused interest There was a faint blush upon her round cheek as she

greeted her old admirer. Mr. Hemstetter shook hands with Johnny in a very friendly way. He was an oldish, impractical man — one of that numerous class of erratic business men who are forever dissatis fied, and seeking a change.

" I am very glad to see you, John — may I call you John ? " he said. Let me thank you for your prompt answer to our postmaster's letter of inquiry. He volunteered to write to you on my behalf. I was looking about for something different in the way of a business in which the profits would be greater. I had noticed in the papers that this coast was receiv ing much attention from investors. I am extremely grateful for your advice to come. I sold out every thing that I possess, and invested the proceeds in as fine a stock of shoes as could be bought in the North. You have a picturesque town here, John. I hope business will be as good as your letter justifies me in expecting."

Johnny's agony was abbreviated by the arrival of Keogh, who hurried up with the news that Mrs. Goodwin would be much pleased to place rooms at the disposal of Mr. Hemstetter and his

daughter. So there Mr. Hemstetter and Rosine were at once conducted and left to recuperate from the fatigue of the voyage, while Johnny went down to see that the cases of shoes were safely stored in the customs warehouse pending their examination by the officials. Keogh, grinning like a shark, skirmished about to find Goodwin, to instruct him not to expose to Mr. Hemstetter the true state of Coralio as a shoe market until Johnny had been given a chance to redeem the situation, if such a thing were possible.

That night the consul and Keogh held a desperate consultation on the breezy porch of the consulate.

"Send 'em back home," began Keogh, reading Johnny's thoughts.

" I would," said Johnny, after a little silence; "but I've been lying to you, Billy."

"All right about that," said Keogh, affably.

"I've told you hundreds of times," said Johnny, slowly, "that I had forgotten that girl, haven't I?"

"About three hundred and seventy-five," admit ted the monument of patience.

"I lied," repeated the consul, "every time. I never forgot her for one minute. I was an obstinate

ass for running away just because she said 'No' once. And I was too proud a fool to go back. I talked with Rosine a few minutes this evening up at Goodwin's. I found out one thing. You re member that farmer fellow who was always after her?"

"Dink Pawson?" asked Keogh.

"Pink Dawson. Well, he wasn't a hill of beans to her. She says she didn't believe a word of the things he told her about me. But I'm sewed up now, Billy. That tomfool letter we sent ruined whatever chance I had left. She'll despise me when she finds out that her old father has been made the victim of a joke that a decent school boy wouldn't have been guilty of. Shoes! Why he couldn't sell twenty pairs of shoes in Coralio if he kept store here for twenty years. You put a pair of shoes on one of these Caribs or Spanish brown boys and what'd he do? Stand on his head and squeal until he'd kicked 'em off. None of 'em ever wore shoes and they never will. If I send 'em back home I'll have to tell the whole story. and what'U she think of me ? I want that girl worse than ever, Billy, and now when

she's in reach I've lost her forever because I tried to

be funny when the thermometer was at 102."

" Keep cheerful," said the optimistic Keogh. " And let 'em open the store. I've been busy myself this

afternoon. We can stir up a temporary boom in

-t> k^*-* ——-- ^tw^, ^*-»-**'

foot-gear anyhow. (I'll buy six pairs when the doors open. I've been around and seen all the fellows and explained the catastrophe. They'll all buy shoes like they was centipedes. Frank Goodwin will take cases of 'em. The Geddies want about eleven pairs between 'em. Clancy is going to invest the savings of weeks, and even old Doc Gregg wants three pairs of alligator-hide slippers if they've got any tens. Blanchard got a look at Miss Hemstetter; and as he's a Frenchman, no less than a dozen pairs will do for him." V ^|U

" A dozen customers," said Johnny, " for a $4,000 stock of shoes! It won't work. There's a big prob lem here to figure out. ^You go home, Billy, and leave me alone. I've got to work at it all by myself. Take that bottle of Three-star along with you — no, sir; not another ounce of booze for the United States consul. I'll sit here to-night and pull out the think

stop. If there's a soft place on this proposition any where I'll land on it. If there isn't there'll be another wreck to the credit of the gorgeous tropics."

Keogh left, feeling that he could be of no use. ^Johnny laid a handful of cigars on a table and stretched himself in a steamer chairj When the sudden daylight broke, silvering the harbour rip ples, he was still sitting there. Then he got up, whistling a little tune, and took his bath.

At nine o'clock he walked down to the dingy little cable office and hung for half an hour over a blank. The result of his application was the following mes sage, which he signed and had transmitted at a cost of $33:

To PINKNEY DAWSON,

Dalesburg, Ala.

Draft for $100 comes to you next mail. Ship me immediately 500 pounds stiff, dry cockleburrs. New use here in arts. Market price twenty cents pound. Further orders likely. Rush.

CHAPTER THIRTEEN

Ships

VVITHIN a week a suitable building had been secured in the Calle Grande, and Mr. Hemstetter's stock of shoes arranged upon their shelves. The rent of the store was moderate; and the stock made a fine showing of neat white boxes, attractively displayed.

Johnny's friends stood by him loyally. On the first day Keogh strolled into the store in a casual kind of way about once every hour, and bought shoes. After he had purchased a pair each of exten sion soles, congress gaiters, button kids, low-quar tered calfs, dancing pumps, rubber boots, tans of various hues, tennis shoes and flowered slippers, he sought but Johnny to be prompted as to the names of

other kinds that he might inquire for. The other English-speaking residents also played their parts nobly by buying often and liberally. Keogh was grand marshal, and made them distribute their patronage, thus keeping up a fair run of custom for several days.

Mr. Hemstetter was gratified by the amount of business done thus far; but expressed surprise that the natives were so backward with their custom.

"Oh, they're awfully shy," explained Johnny, as he wiped his forehead nervously. "They'll get the habit pretty soon. They'll come with a rush when they do come."

One afternoon Keogh dropped into the consul's office, chewing an unlighted cigar thoughtfully.

"Got anything up your sleeve?" he inquired of Johnny. "If you have it's about time to show it. If you can borrow some gent's hat in the audience, and make a lot of customers for an idle stock of shoes come out of it, you'd better spiel. The boys have all laid in enough footwear to last 'em ten years; and there's nothing doing in the shoe store but dolcy far nienty. I just came by there. Your venerable

victim was standing in the door, gazing through his specs at the bare toes passing by his emporium. The natives here have got the true artistic temperament. Me and Clancy took eighteen tintypes this morning in two hours. There's been but one pair of shoes sold all day. Blanchard went in and bought a pair of fur-lined house-slippers because he thought he saw Miss Hemstetter go into the store. I saw him throw the slippers into the lagoon afterwards."

" There's a Mobile fruit steamer coming in to-mor row or next day," said Johnny. " We can't do any thing until then."

" What are you going to do — try to create a de mand?"

"Political economy isn't your strong point," said the consul, impudently. "You can't create a de mand. But you can create a necessity for a demand. That's what I am going to do."

Two weeks after the consul sent his cable, a fruit steamer brought him a huge, mysterious brown bale of some unknown commodity. Johnny's influence with the custom-house people was sufficiently strong for him to get the goods turned over to him without

the usual inspection. He had the bale taken to the consulate and snugly stowed in the back room.

That night he ripped open a corner of it and took out a handful of the cockleburrs. He examined them with the care with which a warrior examines his arms before he goes forth to battle for his lady love and life. The burrs were the ripe August prod uct, as hard as filberts, and bristling with spines as tough and sharp as needles. Johnny whistled softly a little tune, and went out to find Billy Keogh.

Later in the night, when Coralio was steeped in slumber, he and Billy went forth into the deserted streets with their coats bulging like balloons. All up and down the Calle Grande they went, sowing the sharp burrs carefully in the sand, along the narrow sidewalks, in every foot of grass between the silent houses. And then they took the side streets and by ways, missing none. No place where the foot of man, woman or child might fall was slighted. Many trips they made to and from the prickly hoard. And then, nearly at the dawn, they laid themselves down to rest calmly, as great generals do after planning a victory according to the revised tactics, and slept,

knowing that they had sowed with the accuracy of

Satan sowing tares and the perseverance of Paul

planting.

With the rising sun came the purveyors of fruits and meats, and arranged their wares in and around the little market-house. At one end of the town near the seashore the market-house stood; and the sowing of the burrs had not been carried that far. The dealers waited long past the hour when their sales usually began. None came to buy. " Que hay ? " they began to exclaim, one to another.

At their accustomed time, from every 'dobe and palm hut and grass-thatched shack and dim patio glided women — black women, brown women, lemon-colored women, women dun and yellow and tawny. They were the marketers starting to purchase the family supply of cassava, plantains, meat, fowls, and tortillas. Decollete they were and bare-armed and bare-footed, with a single skirt reaching below the knee. Stolid and ox-eyed, they stepped from their doorways into the narrow paths or upon the soft grass of the streets.

The first to emerge uttered ambiguous squeals, and

raised one foot quickly. Another step and they sat down, with shrill cries of alarm, to pick at the new and painful insects that had stung them upon the feet. " Que picadores diablos I " they screeched to one an other across the narrow ways. Some tried the grass instead of the paths, but there they were also stung and bitten by the strange little prickly balls. They plumped down in the grass, and added their lamen tations to those of their sisters in the sandy paths. All through the town was heard the plaint of the feminine jabber. The venders in the market still wondered why no customers came.

Then men, lords of the earth, came forth. They, too, began to hop, to dance, to limp, and to curse. They stood stranded and foolish, or stooped to pluck at the scourge that attacked their feet and ankles. Some loudly proclaimed the pest to be poisonous spiders of an unknown species.

And then the children ran out for their morning romp. And now to the uproar was added the howls of limping infants and cockleburred child hood. Every minute the advancing day brought forth fresh victims.

Dona Maria Castillas y Buenventura de las Casas stepped from her honoured doorway, as was her daily custom, to procure fresh bread from the panaderia across the street. She was clad in a skirt of flowered yellow satin, a chemise of ruffled linen, and wore a purple mantilla from the looms of Spam. Her lemon-tinted feet, alas! were bare. Her progress was ma jestic, for were not her ancestors hidalgos of Aragon ? Three steps she made across the velvety grass, and set her aristocratic sole upon a bunch of Johnny's burrs. Dona Maria Castillas y Buenventura de las Casas emitted a yowl even as a wild-cat. Turning about, she fell upon hands and knees, and crawled — ay, like a beast of the field she crawled back to her honour able door-sill.

Don Senor Udefonso Federico Valdazar, Juez de la Paz, weighing twenty stone, attempted to convey his bulk to the pulperia at the corner of the plaza in order to assuage his matutinal thirst. The first plunge of his unshod foot into the cool grass struck a concealed mine. Don Udefonso fell like a crumbled cathedral, crying out that he had been fatally bitten by a deadly scorpion. Everywhere were the shoeless citizens

hopping, stumbling, limping, and picking from their feet the venomous insects that had come in a single night to harass them.

The first to perceive the remedy was Esteba'n Del-gado, the barber, a man of travel and education. Sit ting upon a stone, he plucked burrs from his toes, and made oration:

"Behold, my friends, these bugs of the devil! I know them well. They soar through the skies in swarms like pigeons. These are dead ones that fell during the night. In Yucatan I have seen them as large as oranges. Yes! There they hiss like ser pents, and have wings like bats. It is the shoes — the shoes that one needs! Zapatos — zapatos para mi 1 "

Esteban hobbled to Mr. Hemstetter's store, and bought shoes. Coming out, he swaggered down the street with impunity, reviling loudly the bugs of the devil. The suffering ones sat up or stood upon one foot and beheld the immune barber. Men, women and children took up the cry: " Zapatos ! zapatos I "

The necessity for the demand had been created. The demand followed. That day Mr. Hemstetter sold three hundred pairs of shoes.

£50 Cabbages and Kings

"It is really surprising," he said to Johnny, who came up in the evening to help him straighten out the stock, " how trade is picking up. Yesterday I made but three sales."

" I told you they'd whoop things up when they got started," said the consul.

" I think I shall order a dozen more cases of goods, to keep the stock up," said Mr. Hemstetter, beaming through his spectacles.

"I wouldn't send in any orders yet," advised Johnny. "Wait till you see how the trade holds up."

Each night Johnny and Keogh sowed the crop that grew dollars by day. At the end of ten days two-thirds of the stock of shoes had been sold ; and the stock of cockleburrs was exhausted. Johnny cabled to Pink Dawson for another 500 pounds, paying twenty cents per pound as before. Mr. Hemstetter carefully made up an order for $1500 worth of shoes from Northern firms. Johnny hung about the store until this order was ready for the mail, and succeed ed in destroying it before it reached the postoffice.

That night he took Rosine under the mango tree by

Goodwin's porch, and confessed everything. She looked him in the eye, and said: "You are a very wicked man. Father and I will go back home. You say it was a joke ? I think it is a very serious mat ter."

But at the end of half an hour's argument the con versation had been turned upon a different subject. The two were considering the respective merits of pale blue and pink wall paper with which the old colonial mansion of the Atwoods in Dalesburg was to be decorated after the wedding.

On the next morning Johnny confessed to Mr. Hemstetter. The shoe merchant put on his specta cles, and said through them: " You strike me as being a most extraordinary young scamp. If I had not managed this enterprise with good business judg ment my entire stock of goods might have been a complete loss. Now, how do you propose to dispose of the rest of it?"

When the second invoice of cockleburrs arrived Johnny loaded them and the remainder of the shoes into a schooner, and sailed down the coast to Alazan,

Cabbages and Kings

There, in the same dark and diabolical manner, he repeated his success: and came back with a bag of money and not so much as a shoestring.

And then he besought his great Uncle of the waving goatee and starred vest to accept his resignation, for the lotus no longer lured him. He hankered for the spinach and cress of Dalesburg.

The services of Mr. William Terence Keogh as acting consul, pro tern., were suggested and accepted, and Johnny sailed with the Hemstetters back to his native shores.

Keogh slipped into the sinecure of the American consulship with the ease that never left him even in such high places. The tintype establishment was soon to become a thing of the past, although its deadly work along the peaceful and helpless Spanish Main was never effaced. The restless partners were about to be off again, scouting ahead of the slow ranks of Fortune. But now they would take different ways. There were rumours of a promising uprising in Peru; and thither the martial Clancy would turn his adven turous steps. As for Keogh, he was figuring in his mind and on quires of Government letter-heads a

scheme that dwarfed the art of misrepresenting the human countenance upon tin.

" What suits me," Keogh used to say, "in the way of a business proposition is something diversified that looks like a longer shot than it is — something in the way of a genteel graft that isn't worked enough for the correspondence schools to be teaching it by mail. I take the long end; but I like to have at least as good a chance to win as a man learning to play poker on an ocean steamer, or running for governor of Texas on the Republican ticket. And when I cash in my winnings I don't want to find any widows' and orphans' chips in my stack."

The grass-grown globe was the green table on which Keogh gambled. The games he played were of his own invention. He was no grubber after the diffident dollar. Nor did he care to follow it with horn and hounds. Rather he loved to coax it with egregious and brilliant flies from its habitat in the waters of strange streams. Yet Keogh was a business man; and his schemes, in spite of their singularity, were as solidly set as the plans of a building contrac tor. In Arthur's time Sir William Keogh would

have been a Knight of the Round Table. In these modern days he rides abroad, seeking the Graft in stead of the Grail.

Three days after Johnny's departure, two small schooners appeared off Coralio. After some delay a boat put off from one of them, and brought a sun burned young man ashore. This young man had a shrewd and calculating eye ; and he gazed with amazement at the strange things that he saw. He found on the beach some one who directed him to the consul's office; and thither he made his way at a nervous gait.

Keogh was sprawled in the official chair, drawing caricatures of his Uncle's head on an official pad of paper. He looked up at his visitor.

"Where's Johnny Atwood?" inquired the sun burned young man, in a business tone.

" Gone," said Keogh, working carefully at Uncle Sam's necktie.

"That's just like him," remarked the nut-brown one, leaning against the table. "He always was a fellow to gallivant around instead of 'tending to business. Will he be in soon ? "

" Don't think so," said Keogh, after a fair amount of deliberation.

" I s'pose he's out at some of his tomfoolery," con jectured the visitor, in a tone of virtuous conviction. " Johnny never would stick to anything long enough to succeed. I wonder how he manages to run his business here, and never be 'round to look after it."

" I'm looking after the business just now," admit ted the pro tern, consul.

"Are you ? — then, say! — where's the factory?" " What factory ? " asked Keogh, with mildly polite interest.

"Why, the factory where they use them cockle-burrs. Lord knows what they use 'em for, anyway! I've got the basements of both them ships out there loaded with 'em. I'll give you a bargain in this lot. I've had every man, woman and child around Dalesburg that wasn't busy pickin' 'em for a month. I hired these ships to bring 'em over. Everybody thought I was crazy. Now, you can have this lot for fifteen cents a pound, delivered on land. And if you want more I guess old Alabam' can come up to the demand. Johnny told me when he left home that if

he struck anything down here that there was any money in he'd let me in on it. Shall I drive the ships in and hitch?"

A look of supreme, almost incredulous, delight dawned in Keogh's ruddy countenance. He dropped his pencil. His eyes turned upon the sunburned young man with joy in them mingled with fear lest his ecstasy should prove a dream.

" For God's sake tell me," said Keogh, earnestly, " are you Dink Pawson ? "

" My name is Pinkney Dawson, ""said the cornerer of the cockleburr market.

Billy Keogh slid rapturously and gently from his chair to his favourite strip of matting on the floor.

There were not many sounds in Coralio on that sultry afternoon. Among those that were may be mentioned a noise of enraptured and unrighteous laughter from a prostrate Irish-American, while a sunburned young man, with a shrewd eye, looked on him with wonder and amazement. Also the " tramp, tramp, tramp " of many welJ-shod feet ip the streets outside. Also the lonesome wash of line waves beat along the historic shores of the Spanish Main,

CHAPTER FOURTEEN

Masters of Arts

A TWO-INCH stub of a blue pencil was the wand with which Keogh performed the preliminary acts of his magic. So, with this he covered paper with dia grams and figures while he waited for the United States of America to send down to Coralio a suc cessor to Atwood, resigned.

The new scheme that his mind had conceived, his stout heart indorsed, and his blue pencil corrobo rated, was laid around the characteristics and human frailties of the new president of Anchuria. These characteristics, and the situation out of which Keogh hoped to wrest a golden tribute, deserve chronicling contributive to the clear order of events.

President Losada — many called him Dictator —

was a man whose genius would have made him con spicuous even among Anglo-Saxons, had not that genius been intermixed with other traits that were petty and subversive. He had some of the lofty pa triotism of Washington (the man he most admired), the force of Napoleon, and much of the wisdom of the sages. These characteristics might have justified him in the assumption of the title of " The Illustrious Liberator," had they not been accompanied by a stupendous and amazing vanity that kept him in the less worthy ranks of the dictators.

Yet he did his country great service. With a mighty grasp he shook it nearly free from the shackles of ignorance and sloth and the vermin that fed upon it, and all but made it a power in the council of nations. He established schools and hospitals, built roads, bridges, railroads and palaces, and bestowed generous subsidies upon the arts and sciences. He was the absolute despot and the idol of his people. The wealth of the country poured into his hands. Other presidents had been rapacious without reason. Losada amassed enormous wealth, but his people had their share of the benefits.

The joint in his armour was his insatiate passion for monuments and tokens commemorating his glory. In every town he caused to be erected statues of himself bearing legends in praise of his greatness. In the walls of every public edifice, tablets were fixed reciting his splendour and the gratitude of his subjects. His statuettes and portraits were scattered through out the land in every house and hut. One of the sycophants in his court painted him as St. John, with a halo and a train of attendants in full uniform. Losada saw nothing incongruous in this picture, and had it hung in a church in the capital. He ordered from a French sculptor a marble group including himself with Napoleon, Alexander the Great, and one or two others whom he deemed worthy of the honour.

He ransacked Europe for decorations, employing policy, money and intrigue to cajole the orders he cov eted from kings and rulers. On state occasions his breast was covered from shoulder to shoulder with crosses, stars, golden roses, medals and ribbons. It was said that the man who could contrive for him a new decoration, or invent some new method of extoll-ing his greatness, might plunge a hand deep into the treasury.

This was the man upon whom Billy Keogh had his eye. The gentle buccaneer had observed the rain of favours that fell upon those who ministered to the president's vanities, and he did not deem it his duty to hoist his umbrella against the scattering drops of liquid fortune.

In a few weeks the new consul arrived, releasing Keogh from his temporary duties. He was a young man fresh from college, who lived for botany alone. The consulate at Coralio ga.ve him the opportunity to study tropical flora. He wore smoked glasses, and carried a green umbrella. He filled the cool, back porch of the consulate with plants and specimens so that space for a bottle and chair was not to be found. Keogh gazed on him sadly, but without rancour, and began to pack his gripsack. For his new plot against stagnation along the Spanish Main required of him a voyage overseas.

Soon came the Karlsefin again — she of the trampish habits — gleaning a cargo of cocoanuts for a speculative descent upon the New York market. Keogh was booked for a passage on the return trip.

" Yes, I'm going to New York," he explained to the group of his countrymen that had gathered on the beach to see him off. " But I'll be back before you miss me. I've undertaken the art education of this piebald country, and I'm not the man to desert it while it's in the early throes of tintypes."

With this mysterious declaration of his intentions Keogh boarded the Karlsefin.

Ten days later, shivering, with the collar of his thin coat turned high, he burst into the studio of Carolus White at the top of a tall building in Tenth Street, New York City.

Carolus White was smoking a cigarette and frying sausages over an oil stove. He was only twenty-three, and had noble theories about art.

"Billy Keogh!" exclaimed White, extending the hand that was not busy with the frying pan. " From what part of the uncivilized world, I wonder!"

"Hello, Carry," said Keogh, dragging"forward a stool, and holding his fingers close to the stove. " I'm glad I found you so soon. I've been looking for you

all day in the directories and art galleries. The free-lunch man on the corner told me where you were, quick. I was sure you'd be painting pictures yet."

Keogh glanced about the studio with the shrewd eye of a connoisseur in business.

"Yes, you can do it," he declared, with many gentle nods of his head. "That big one in the corner with the angels and green clouds and band wagon is just the sort of thing we want. What would you call that, Carry — scene from Coney Island, aint it?"

"That," said White, "I had intended to call 'The Translation of Elijah/ but you may be nearer right than I am."

" Name doesn't matter," said Keogh, largely; " it's the frame and the varieties of paint that does the trick. Now, I can tell you in a minute what I want. I've come on a little voyage of two thousand miles to take you in with me on a scheme. I thought of you as soon as the scheme showed itself to me. How would you like to go back with me and paint a pic ture ? Ninety days for the trip, and five thousand dollars for the job."

" Cereal food or hair-tonic posters ? " asked White.

"It isn't an ad."

" What kind of a picture is it to be ? "

" It's a long story," said Keogh.

"Go ahead with it. If you don't mind, while you talk I'll just keep my eye on these sausages. Let 'em get one shade deeper than a Vandyke brown and you spoil 'em."

Keogh explained his project. They were to return to Coralio, where White was to pose as a distin guished American portrait painter who was touring in the tropics as a relaxation from his arduous and remunerative professional labours. It was not an unreasonable hope, even to those who trod in the beaten paths of business, that an artist with so much prestige might secure a commission to per petuate upon canvas the lineaments of the president, and secure a share of the pesos that were raining upon the caterers to his weaknesses.

Keogh had set his price at ten thousand dollars. Artists had been paid more for portraits. He and White were to share the expenses of the trip, and divide the possible profits. Thus he laid the scheme

before White, whom he had known in the West

before one declared for Art and the other became a

Bedouin.

Before long the two machinators abandoned the rigour of the bare studio for a snug corner of a cafe. There they sat far into the night, with old envelopes and Keogh's stub of blue pencil between them.

At twelve o'clock White doubled up in his chair, with his chin on his fist, and shut his eyes at the unbeautiful wall-paper.

"I'll go you, Billy," he said, in the quiet tones of decision. " I've got two or three hundred saved up for sausages and rent; and I'll take the chance with you. Five thousand! It will give me two years in Paris and one in Italy. I'll begin to pack to-mor row."

" You'll begin in ten minutes," said Keogh. " It's to-morrow now. The Karlsefin starts back at four p. M. Come on to your painting shop, and I'll help you."

For five months in the year Coralio is the Newport of Anchuria. Then only does the town possess life. From November to March it is practically the seat of

government. The president with his official family sojourns there; and society follows him. The pleas ure-loving people make the season one long holiday of amusement and rejoicing. Fiestas, balls, games, sea bathing, processions and small theatres contrib ute to their enjoyment. The famous Swiss band from the capital plays in the little plaza every even ing, while the fourteen carriages and vehicles in the town circle in funereal but complacent procession. Indians from the interior mountains, looking like prehistoric stone idols, come down to peddle their handiwork in the streets. The people throng the narrow ways, a chattering, happy, careless stream of buoyant humanity. Preposterous children rigged out with the shortest of ballet skirts and gilt wings, howl, underfoot, among the effervescent crowds. Especially is the arrival of the presidential party, at the opening of the season, attended with pomp, show and patriotic demonstrations of enthusiasm and delight.

When Keogh and White reached their destination, on the return trip of the Karlsefin, the gay winter sea son was well begun. As they steoped upon the

beach they could hear the band playing in the plaza. The village maidens, with fireflies already fixed in their dark locks, were gliding, barefoot and coy-eyed, along the paths. Dandies in white linen, swinging their canes, were beginning their seductive strolls. The air was full of human essence, of arti ficial enticement, of coquetry, indolence, pleasure — the man-made sense of existence.

The first two or three days after their arrival were spent in preliminaries. Keogh escorted the artist about town, introducing him to the little circle of English-speaking residents and pulling whatever wires he could to effect the spreading of White's fame as a painter. And then Keogh planned a more spec tacular demonstration of the idea he wished to keep before the public.

He and White engaged rooms in the Hotel de los Estranjeros. The two were clad in new suits of immaculate duck, with American straw hats, and carried canes of remarkable uniqueness and inutility. Few caballeros in Coralio — even the gorgeously uni formed officers of the Anchurian army — were as conspicuous for ease and elegance of demeanour as

Keogh and his friend, the great American painter, Senor White.

White set up his easel on the beach and made strik ing sketches of the mountain and sea views. The native population formed at his rear in a vast, chat tering semicircle to watch his work. Keogh, with his care for details, had arranged for himself a pose which he carried out with fidelity. His role was that of friend to the great artist, a man of affairs and leisure. The visible emblem of his position was a pocket camera.

"For branding the man who owns it," said he, "a genteel dilettante with a bank account and an easy conscience, a steam-yacht aint in it with a camera. You see a man doing nothing but loafing around making snap-shots, and you know right away he reads up well in 'Bradstreet.' You notice these old millionaire boys — soon as they get through taking everything else in sight they go to taking photographs. People are more impressed by a kodak than they are by a title or a four-carat scarf-pin." So Keogh strolled blandly about Coralio, snapping the scenery and the shrinking

sefioritas, while White posed conspicuously in the
higher regions of art.

Two weeks after their arrival, the scheme began to bear fruit. An aide-de-camp of the president drove to the hotel in a dashing victoria. The president desired that Senor White come to the Casa Morena for an informal interview.

Keogh gripped his pipe tightly between his teeth. " Not a cent less than ten thousand," he said to the artist — " remember the price. And in gold or its equivalent — don't let him stick you with this bar gain-counter stuff they call money here."

"Perhaps it isn't that he wants," said White.

" Get out!" said Keogh, with splendid confidence. "I know what he wants. He wants his picture painted by the celebrated young American painter and filibuster now sojourning in his down-trodden country. Off you go."

The victoria sped away with the artist. Keogh walked up and down, puffing great clouds of smoke from his pipe, and waited. In an hour the victoria swept again to the door of the hotel, deposited White, and vanished. The artist dashed up the stairs,
three at a step. Keogh stopped smoking, and be came a silent interrogation point.

" Landed," exclaimed White, with his boyish face flushed with elation. " Billy, you are a wonder. He wants a picture. I'll tell you all about it. By Heavens! that dictator chap is a corker! He's a dictator clear down to his finger-ends. He's a kind of combination of Julius Csesar, Lucifer and Chaun-cey Depew done in sepia. Polite and grim — that's his way. The room I saw him in was about ten acres big, and looked like a Mississippi steamboat with its gilding and mirrors and white paint. He talks English better than I can ever hope to. The matter of the price came up. I mentioned ten thousand. I expected him to call the guard and have me taken out and shot. He didn't move an eyelash. He just waved one of his chestnut hands in a careless way, and said, * Whatever you say.' I am to go back to morrow and discuss with him the details of the picture."

Keogh hung his head. Self-abasement was easy to read in his downcast countenance.

"I'm failing. Carry," he said, sorrowfully. "I'm
£70 Cabbages and Kings
not fit to handle these man's-size schemes any longer. Peddling oranges in a push-cart is about the suitable graft for me. When I said ten thousand, I swear I thought I had sized up that brown man's limit to within two cents. He'd have melted down for fifteen thousand just as easy. Say — Carry — you'll see old man Keogh safe in some nice, quiet idiot asylum, won't you, if he makes a break like that again?" •

The Casa Morena, although only one story in height, was a building of brown stone, luxurious as a palace in its interior. It stood on a low hill in a walled garden of splendid tropical flora at the upper edge of Coralio. The next day the president's car riage came again for the artist. Keogh went out for a walk along the beach, where he and his "picture box" were now familiar sights. When he returned to the hotel White was sitting in a steamer-chair on the balcony.

" Well," said Keogh, " did you and His Nibs decide on the kind of a chromo he wants ? "

White got up and walked back and forth on the balcony a few times. Then he stopped, and laughed
strangely. His face was flushed, and his eyes were bright with a kind of angry amusement.

"Look here, Billy," he said, somewhat roughly, " when you first came to me in my studio and men tioned a picture, I thought you wanted a Smashed Oats or a Hair Tonic poster painted on a range of mountains or the side of a continent. Well, either of those jobs would have been

Art in its highest form compared to the one you've steered me against. I can't paint that picture, Billy. You've got to let me out. Let me try to tell you what that barbarian wants. He had it all planned out and even a sketch made of his idea. The old boy doesn't draw badly at all. But, ye goddesses of Art! listen to the mon strosity he expects me to paint. He wants himself in the centre of the canvas, of course. He is to be painted as Jupiter sitting on Olympus, with the clouds at his feet. At one side of him stands George Washington, in full regimentals, with his hand on the president's shoulder. An angel with outstretched wings hovers overhead, and is placing a laurel wreath on the president's head, crowning him — Queen of the May, I suppose. In the background is to be

Cabbages and Kings cannon, more angels and soldiers. The man who would paint that picture would have to have the soul of a dog, and would deserve to go down into oblivion without even a tin can tied to his tail to sound his memory."

Little beads of moisture crept out all over Billy Keogh's brow. The stub of his blue pencil had not figured out a contingency like this. The machinery of his plan had run with flattering smoothness until now. He dragged another chair upon the balcony, and got White back to his seat. He lit his pipe with apparent calm.

"Now, sonny," he said, with gentle grimness, "you and me will have an Art to Art talk. You've got your art and I've got mine. Yours is the real Pierian stuff that turns up its nose at bock-beer signs and oleographs of the Old Mill. Mine's the art of Business. This was my scheme, and it worked out like two-and-two. Paint that president man as Old King Cole, or Venus, or a landscape, or a fresco, or a bunch of lilies, or anything he thinks he looks like. But get the paint on the canvas and collect the spoils. You wouldn't throw me down,

Carry, at this stage of the game. Think of that ten thousand."

" I can't help thinking of it," said White, and that's what hurts. I'm tempted to throw every ideal I ever had down in the mire, and steep my soul in infamy by painting that picture. That five thousand meant three years of foreign study to me, and I'd almost sell my soul for that."

" Now it ain't as bad as that," said Keogh, sooth ingly. "It's a business proposition. It's so much paint and time against money. I don't fall in with your idea that that picture would so everlastingly jolt the art side of the question. George Washington was all right, you know, and nobody could say a word against the angel. I don't think so bad of that group. If you was to give Jupiter a pair of epaulets and a sword, and kind of work the clouds around to look like a blackberry patch, it wouldn't make such a bad battle scene. WTiy, if we hadn't already settled on the price, he ought to pay an extra thousand for Washington, and the angel ought to raise it five hun dred."

"You don't understand, Billy," said White, with

an uneasy laugh "Some of us fellows who try to paint have big notions about Art. I wanted to paint a picture some day that people would stand before and forget that it was made of paint. I wanted it to creep into them like a bar of music and mushroom there like a soft bullet. And I wanted 'em to go away and ask, 'What else has he done? 5 And I didn't want 'em to find a thing; not a portrait nor a magazine cover nor an illustration nor a drawing of a girl — nothing but the picture. That's why I've lived on fried sausages, and tried to keep true to myself. I persuaded myself to do this portrait for the chance it might give me to study abroad. But this howling, screaming caricature! Good Lord! can't you see how it is ? "

"Sure," said Keogh, as tenderly as he would have spoken to a child, and he laid a long forefinger on White's knee. "I see. It's bad to have your art all slugged up like that. I know. You wanted to paint a big thing like the panorama of the battle of Gettysburg. But let me kalsomine you a little men tal sketch to consider. Up to date we're out $385.50 on this scheme. Our capital took every cent both

of us could raise. We've got about enough left to get back to New York on. I need my share of that ten thousand. I want to work a copper deal in Idaho, and make a hundred thousand. That's the business end of the thing. Come down off your art perch, Carry, and let's land that hatful of dollars."

"Billy," said White, with an effort, "I'll try. I won't say I'll do it, but I'll try. I'll go at it, and put it through if I can."

"That's business," said Keogh, heartily. "Good boy! Now, here's another thing — rush that picture — crowd it through as quick as you can. Get a couple of boys to help you mix the paint if necessary. I've picked up some pointers around town. The people here are beginning to get sick of Mr. President. They say he's been too free with concessions; and they accuse him of trying to make a dicker with Eng land to sell out the country. We want that picture done and paid for before there's any row."

In the great patio of Casa Morena, the president caused to be stretched a huge canvas. Under this White set up his temporary studio. For two hours each day the great man sat to him.

£76 Cabbages and Kings

White worked faithfully. But, as the work pro gressed, he had seasons of bitter scorn, of infinite self-contempt, of sullen gloom and sardonic gaiety. Keogh, with the patience of a great general, soothed, coaxed, argued — kept him at the picture.

At the end of a month White announced that the picture was completed — Jupiter, Washington, an gels, clouds, cannon and all. His face was pale and his mouth drawn straight when he told Keogh. He said the president was much pleased with it. It was to be hung in the National Gallery of Statesmen and Heroes. The artist had been requested to return to Casa Morena on the following day to receive pay ment. At the appointed time he left the hotel, silent under his friend's joyful talk of their success.

An hour later he walked into the room where Keogh was waiting, threw his hat on the floor, and sat upon the table.

" Billy," he said, in strained and labouring tones, " I've a little money out West in a small business that my brother is running. It's what I've been living on while I've been studying art. I'll draw out my share and pay you back what you've lost on this scheme."

" Lost!" exclaimed Keogh, jumping up. " Didn't you get paid for the picture ? "

"Yes, I got paid," said White. "But just now there isn't any picture, and there isn't any pay. If you care to hear about it, here are the edifying de tails. The president and I were looking at the paint ing. His secretary brought a bank draft on New York for ten thousand dollars and handed it to me. The moment I touched it I went wild. I tore it into little pieces and threw them on the floor. A work man was repainting the pillars inside the patio. A bucket of his paint happened to be convenient. I picked up his brush and slapped a quart of blue paint all over that ten-thousand-dollar nightmare. I bowed, and walked out. The president didn't move or speak. That was one time he was taken by surprise. It's tough on you, Billy, but I couldn't help it."

There seemed to be excitement in Coralio. Out side there was a confused, rising murmur pierced by high-pitched cries. " Bajo el traidw — Muerte el traidor I " were the words they seemed to form.

"Listen to that!" exclaimed White, bitterly; "I know that much Spanish. They're shouting, e Down

with the traitor!' I heard them before. I felt that they meant me. I was a traitor to Art. The picture had to go."

" ' Down with the blank fool' would have suited your case better/' said Keogh, with fiery emphasis. "You tear up ten thousand dollars like an old rag because the way you've spread on five dollars' worth of paint hurts your conscience. Next time I pick a side-partner in a scheme the man has got to go before a notary and swear he never even heard the word ' ideal' mentioned."

Keogh strode from the room, white-hot. White paid little attention to his resentment. The scorn of Billy Keogh seemed a trifling thing beside the greater self-scorn he had escaped.

In Coralio the excitement waxed. An outburst was imminent. The cause of this demonstration of displeasure was the presence in the town of a big, pink-cheeked Englishman, who, it was said, was an agent of his government come to clinch the bargain by which the president placed his people in the hands of a foreign power. It was charged that not only had he given away priceless eoncessions, but that the

public debt was to be transferred into the hands of the English, and the custom-houses turned over to them as a guarantee. The long-enduring people had determined to make their protest felt.

On that night, in Coralio and in other towns, their ire found vent. Yelling mobs, mercurial but danger ous, roamed the streets. They overthrew the great bronze statue of the president that stood in the cen tre of the plaza, and hacked it to shapeless pieces. They tore from public buildings the tablets set there proclaiming the glory of the " Illustrious Liberator." His pictures in the government offices were demol ished. The mobs even attacked the Casa Morena, but were driven away by the military, which remained faithful to the executive. All the night terror reigned.

The greatness of Losada was shown by the fact that by noon the next day order was restored, and he was still absolute. He issued proclamations deny ing positively that any negotiation of any kind had been entered into with England. Sir Stafford Vaughn, the pink-cheeked Englishman, also declared in plac ards and in public print that his presence there had

£80 Cabbages and Kings

no international significance. He was a traveller without guile. In fact (so he stated), he had not even spoken with the president or been in his presence since his arrival.

During this disturbance, White was preparing for his homeward voyage in the steamship that was to sail within two or three days. About noon, Keogh, the restless, took his camera out with the hope of speeding the lagging hours. The town was now as quiet as if peace had never departed from her perch on the red-tiled roofs.

About the middle of the afternoon, Keogh hurried back to the hotel with something decidedly special in his air. He retired to the little room where he de veloped his pictures.

Later on he came out to White on the balcony, with a luminous, grim, predatory smile on his face.

" Do you know what that is ? " he asked, holding up a 4 x 5 photograph mounted on cardboard.

" Snap-shot of a senorita sitting in the sand — allit eration unintentional," guessed White, lazily.

<l Wrong," said Keogh with shining eyes. "It's a slung-shot. It's a can of dynamite. It's a gold

mine. It's a sight draft on your president man for twenty thousand dollars — yes, sir — twenty thou sand this time, and no spoiling the picture. No ethics of art in the way. Art! You with your smelly little tubes! I've got you skinned to death with a kodak. Tak - a look at that."

White took the picture in his hand, and gave a long whistle.

" Jove!" he exclaimed, "but wouldn't that stir up a row in town if you let it be seen. How in the world did you get it, Billy?"

"You know that high wall around the president man's back garden? I was up there trying to get a bird's-eye of the town. I happened to notice a chink in the wall where a stone and a lot of plaster had slid out. Thinks I, I'll take a peep through to see how Mr. President's cabbages are growing. The first thing I saw was him and this Sir Englishman sit-ting at a little table about twenty feet away. They had the table all spread over with documents, and they were hobnobbing over them as thick as two pirates. 'Twas a nice corner of the garden, all private and shady with palms and orange trees, and

Cabbages and Kings they had a pail of champagne set by handy in the grass. I knew then was the time for me to make my big hit in Art. So I raised the machine up to the crack, and pressed the button. Just as I did so them old boys shook hands on the deal — you see they took that way in the picture."

Keogh put on his coat and hat.

" What are you going to do with it ? " asked White.

" Me," said Keogh in a hurt tone, " why, I'm going to tie a pink ribbon to it and hang it on the what-not, of course. I'm surprised at you. But while I'm out you just try to figure out what ginger-cake potentate would be most likely to want to buy this work of art for his private collection — just to keep it out of circulation."

The sunset was reddening the tops of the cocoanut palms when Billy Keogh came back from Casa Mo-rena. He nodded to the artist's questioning gaze; and lay down on a cot with his hands under the back of his head.

" I saw him. He paid the money like a little man. They didn't want to let me in at first. I told 'em it was important. Yes, that president man is on the

plenty-able list. He's got a beautiful business system about the way he uses his brains. ^All I had to do was to hold up the photograph so he could see it, and name the price. He just smiled, and walked over to a safe and got the cash. Twenty one-thousand-dol lar brand-new United States Treasury notes he laid on the table, like I'd pay out a dollar and a quarter. Fine notes, too — they crackled with a sound like burning the brush off a ten-acre lot."

" Let's try the feel of one," said White, curiously. " I never saw a thousand-dollar bill." Keogh did not immediately respond.

" Carry," he said, in an absent-minded way, ft you think a heap of your art, don't you ? "

" More," said White, frankly, " than has been for the financial good of myself and my friends."

" I thought you were a fool the other day," went on Keogh, quietly, "and I'm not sure now that you wasn't. But if you was, so am I. I've been in some funny deals, Carry, but I've always managed to scramble fair, and match my brains and capital against the other fellow's. But when it comes to — well, when you've got the other fellow cinched, and the

screws on him, and he's got to put up — why, it don't strike me as being a man's game. They've got a name for it, you know; it's — confound you, don't you un derstand. A fellow feels — it's something like that blamed art of yours — he — well, I tore that photo graph up and laid the pieces on that stack of money and shoved the whole business back across the table. * Excuse me, Mr. Losada,' I said, ' but I guess I've made a mistake in the price. You get the photo for nothing.' Now, Carry, you get out the pencil, and we'll do some more figuring. I'd like to save enough out of our capital for you to have some fried sausages in your joint when you get back to

New York."

CHAPTER FIFTEEN

Dicky

1 HERE is little consecutiveness along the Spanish Main. Things happen there intermittently. Even Time seems to hang his scythe daily on the branch of an orange tree while he takes a siesta and a cigarette.

After the ineffectual revolt against the administra tion of President Losada, the country settled again into quiet toleration of the abuses with which he had been charged. In Coralio old political enemies went arm-in-arm, lightly eschewing for the time all differ ences of opinion.

The failure of the art expedition did not stretch the cat-footed Keogh upon his back. The ups and downs of Fortune made smooth travelling for his nimble steps. His blue pencil stub was at work again be-

fore the smoke of the steamer on which White sailed had cleared away from the horizon. He had but to speak a word to Geddie to find his credit negotiable for whatever goods he wanted from the store of Brannigan & Company. On the same day on which White arrived in New York Keogh, at the rear of a train of five pack mules loaded with hardware and cutlery, set his face toward the grim, interior moun tains. There the Indian tribes wash gold dust from the auriferous streams; and when a market is brought to them trading is brisk and muy bueno in the Cor dilleras.

In Coralio Time folded his wings and paced weari ly along his drowsy path. They who had most cheered the torpid hours were gone. Clancy had sailed on a Spanish barque for Colon, contemplating a cut across the isthmus and then a further voyage to end at Callao, where the fighting was said to be on. Geddie, whose quiet and genial nature had once served to mitigate the frequent dull reaction of lotus eating, was now a home-man, happy with his bright orchid, Paula, and never even dreaming of or regret ting the unsolved, sealed and monogramed Bottle,

whose contents, now inconsiderable, were held safely in the keeping of the sea.

Well may the Walrus, most discerning and eclectic of beasts, place sealing-wax midway on his pro gramme of topics that fall pertinent and diverting upon the ear.

Atwood was gone — he of the hospitable back porch and ingenuous cunning. Dr. Gregg, with his trepanning story smouldering within him, was a whiskered volcano, always showing signs of immi nent eruption, and was not to be considered in the ranks of those who might contribute to the ameliora tion of ennui. The new consul's note chimed with the sad sea waves and the violent tropical greens — he had not a bar of Scheherezade or of the Round Table in his lute. Goodwin was employed with large projects: what time he was loosed from them found him at his home, where he loved to be. There fore it will be seen that there was a dearth of fellow ship and entertainment among the foreign contingent of Coralio.

And then Dicky Maloney dropped down from the clouds upon the town, and amused it.

Nobody knew where Dicky Maloney hailed from or how he reached Coralio. He appeared there one day; and that was all. He afterward said that he came on the fruit steamer Thor; but an inspection of the Thor's passenger list of that date was found to be Maloneyless. Curiosity, however, soon perished; and Dicky took his place among the odd fish cast up by the Caribbean.

He was an active, devil-may-care, rollicking fellow with an engaging gray eye, the most irresistible grin, a rather dark or much sunburned complexion, and a head of the fieriest red hair ever seen in that country. Speaking the Spanish language as well as he spoke English, and seeming always to have plenty of silver in his pockets, it was not long before he was a wel come companion whithersoever he went. He had an extreme fondness for vino bianco, and gained the rep utation of being able to drink more of it than any three men in town. Everybody called him " Dicky "; everybody cheered up at the sight of him — especially the natives, to whom his marvellous red hair and his free-and-easy style were a constant delight and envy. Wherever you Tvent in the town you would soon see

Dicky or hear his genial laugh, and find around him a group of admirers who appreciated him both for his good nature and the white wine he was always so ready to buy.

A considerable amount of speculation was had con cerning the object of his sojourn there, until one day he silenced this by opening a small shop for the sale of tobacco, dulces and the handiwork of the interior Indians — fibre-and-silk-woven goods, deerskin za-patos and basketwork of tide reeds. Even then he did not change his habits; for he was drinking and playing cards half the day and night with the coman-dante, the collector of customs, the Jeje Politico and other gay dogs among the native officials.

One day Dicky saw Pasa, the daughter of Mada-ma Ortiz, sitting in the side-door of the Hotel des los Estranjeros. He stopped in his tracks, still, for the first time in Coralio; and then he sped, swift as a deer, to find Vasquez, a gilded native youth, to present him.

The young men had named Pasa "La Santita Naranjadita. " Naranjadita is a Spanish word for a certain colour that you must go to more trouble to describe in English. By saying "The little saint.

tinted the most beautiful-delicate-slightly-orange-golden," you will approximate the description of Madama Ortiz's daughter.

La Madama Ortiz sold rum in addition to other liquors. Now, you must know that the rum expiates whatever opprobrium attends upon the other com modities. For rum-making, mind you, is a gov ernment monopoly; and to keep a government dispensary assures respectability if not preeminence. Moreover, the saddest of precisians could find no fault with the conduct of the shop. Customers drank there in the lowest of spirits and fearsomely, as in the shadow of the dead; for Madama's ancient and vaunted lineage counteracted even the rum's behest to be merry. For, was she not of the Iglesias, who landed with Pizarro ? And had not her deceased husband been comisionado de caminos y puentes for the district ?

In the evenings Pasa sat by the window in the room next to the one where they drank, and strummed dreamily upon her guitar. And then, by twos and threes, would come visiting young caballeros and oc cupy the prim line of chairs set against the wall of this

room. They were there to besiege the heart of " La Santita. " Their method (which is not proof against intelligent competition) consisted of expanding the chest, looking valorous, and consuming a gross or two of cigarettes. Even saints delicately oranged pre fer to be wooed differently.

Dona Pasa would tide over the vast chasms of nico-tinized silence with music from her guitar, while she wondered if the romances she had read about gallant and more — more contiguous cavaliers were all lies. At somewhat regular intervals Madama would glide in from the dispensary with a sort of drought-sug gesting gleam in her eye, and there would be a rustling of stiffly-starched white trousers as one of the caballeros would propose an adjournment to the bar.

That Dicky Maloney would, sooner or later, ex plore this field was a thing to be foreseen.

There were few doors in Coralio into which his red head had not been poked.

In an incredibly short space of time after his first sight of her he was there, seated close beside her rock ing chair. There were no back-against-the-wall

poses in Dicky's theory of wooing. His plan of sub jection was an attack at close range. To carry the fortress with one concentrated, ardent, eloquent, ir resistible escalade — that was Dicky's way.

Pasa was descended from the proudest Spanish families in the country. Moreover, she had had unusual advantages. Two years in a New Orleans school had elevated her ambitions and fitted her for a fate above the ordinary maidens of her native land. And yet here she succumbed to the first red-haired scamp with a glib tongue and a charming smile that came along and courted her properly.

Very soon Dicky took her to the little church on the corner of the plaza, and " Mrs. Maloney " was added to her string of distinguished names.

And it was her fate to sit, with her patient, saintly eyes and figure like a bisque Psyche, behind the se questered counter of the little shop, while Dicky drank and philandered with his frivolous acquaintances.

The women, with their naturally fine instinct, saw a chance for vivisection, and delicately taunted her with his habits. She turned upon them in a beauti ful, steady blaze of sorrowful contempt.

"You meat-cows," she said, in her level, crystal-clear tones; "you know nothing of a man. Your men are maromeros. They are fit only to roll ciga rettes in the shade until the sun strikes and shrivels them up. They drone in your hammocks and you comb their hair and feed them with fresh fruit. My man is of no such blood. Let him drink of the wine. When he has taken sufficient of it to drown one of your flaccitos he will come home to me more of a man than one thousand of your pobrecitos. My hair he smoothes and braids; to me he sings; he himself re moves my zapatos, and there, there, upon each instep leaves a kiss. He holds — Oh, you will never understand! Blind ones who have never known a man."

Sometimes mysterious things happened at night about Dicky's shop. While the front of it was dark, in the little room back of it Dicky and a few of his friends would sit about a table carrying on some kind of very quiet negocios until quite late. Finally he would let them out the front door very carefully, and go upstairs to his little saint. These visitors were generally conspirator-like men with dark clothes and

£94 Cabbages and Kings

hats. Of course, these dark doings were noticed

after a while, and talked about.

Dicky seemed to care nothing at all for the society of the alien residents of the town. He avoided Good win, and his skilful escape from the trepanning story of Dr. Gregg is still referred to, in Coralio, as a mas terpiece of lightning diplomacy.

Many letters arrived, addressed to "Mr. Dicky Maloney," or " Senor Dickee Maloney," to the con siderable pride of Pasa. That so many people should desire to write to him only confirmed her own suspi cion that the light from his red head shone around the world. As to their contents she never felt curiosity. There was a wife for you!

The one mistake Dicky made in Coralio was to run out of money at the wrong time. Where his money came from was a puzzle, for the sales of his shop were next to nothing, but that source failed, and at a pe culiarly unfortunate time. It was when the coman-dante, Don Senor el Coronel Encarnacion Rios, looked upon the little saint seated in the shop and felt his heart go pitapat.

The comandante, who was versed in all the intri-
cate arts of gallantry, first delicately hinted at his sen timents by donning his dress
uniform and strutting up and down fiercely before her window. Pasa, glancing demurely with her
saintly eyes, instantly per ceived his resemblance to her parrot, Chichi, and was diverted to the
extent of a smile. The comandante saw the smile, which was not intended for him. Con vinced of
an impression made, he entered the shop, confidently, and advanced to open compliment. Pasa
froze; he pranced; she flamed royally; he was charmed to injudicious persistence; she
commanded him to leave the shop; he tried to capture her hand, and — Dicky entered, smiling
broadly, full of white wine and the devil.

He spent five minutes in punishing the comandante scientifically and carefully, so that
the pain might be prolonged as far as possible. At the end of that time he pitched the rash wooer
out the door upon the stones of the street, senseless.

A barefooted policeman who had been watching the affair from across the street blew a
whistle. A squad of four soldiers came running from the cuartel around the corner When they
saw that the offender
was Dicky, they stopped, and blew more whistles, which brought out reinforcements of
eight. Deem ing the odds against them sufficiently reduced, the military advanced upon the
disturber.

Dicky, being thoroughly imbued with the martial spirit, stooped and drew the
comandantes sword, which was girded about him, and charged his foe* He chased the standing
army four squares, playfully prodding its squealing rear and hacking at its ginger-coloured heels.

But he was not so successful with the civic authori ties* Six muscular, nimble policemen
overpowered him and conveyed him, triumphantly but warily, to jail. "El Diablo Colorado 19
they dubbed him, and derided the military for its defeat.

Dicky, with the rest of the prisoners, could look out through the barred door at the grass
of the little plaza, at a row of orange trees and the red tile roofs and 'dobe walls of a line of
insignificant stores.

At sunset along a path across this plaza came a melancholy procession of sad-faced
women bearing plantains, cassaba, bread and fruit — each coming with food to some wretch
behind those bars to whom
she still clung and furnished the means of life. Twice a day — morning and evening —
they were permitted to come. Water was furnished to her compulsory guests by the republic, but
no food.

That evening Dicky's name was called by the sen try, and he stepped before the bars of
the door. There stood his little saint, a black mantilla draped about her head and shoulders, her
face like glorified melan choly, her clear eyes gazing longingly at him as if they might draw him
between the bars to her. She brought a chicken, some oranges, dulces and a loaf of white bread.
A soldier inspected the food, and passed it in to Dicky. Pasa spoke calmly, as she always did, and
briefly, in her thrilling, flute-like tones. " An gel of my life," she said, " let it not be long that
thou art away from me. Thou knowest that life is not a thing to be endured with thou not at my
side. Tell me if I can do aught in this matter. If not, I will wait — a little while. I come again in
the morning. "

Dicky, with his shoes removed so as not to disturb his fellow prisoners, tramped the floor
of the jail half the night condemning his lack of money and the cause of it — whatever that
might have been. He

knew very well that money would have bought his re lease at once.

For two days succeeding Pasa came at the appoint ed times and brought him food. He eagerly inquired each time if a letter or package had come for him, and she mournfully shook her head.

On the morning of the third day she brought only a small loaf of bread. There were dark circles under her eyes. She seemed as calm as ever.

" By jingo," said Dicky, who seemed to speak in English or Spanish as the whim seized him, " this is dry provender, muchachita. Is this the best you can dig up for a fellow ? "

Pasa looked at him as a mother looks at a beloved but capricious babe.

"Think better of it," she said, in a low voice; " since for the next meal there will be nothing. The last centavo is spent." She pressed closer against the grating.

" Sell the goods in the shop — take anything for them."

" Have I not tried ? Did I not offer them for one-tenth their cost ? Not even one peso would any one

give. There is not one real in this town to assist Dickee Malonee."

Dick clenched his teeth grimly. " That's the co-mandante, " he growled. " He's responsible for that sentiment. Wait, oh, wait till the cards are all out. "

Pasa lowered her voice to almost a whisper. " And, listen, heart of my heart," she said, " I have endeav oured to be brave, but I cannot live without thee. Three days now— "

Dicky caught a faint gleam of steel from the folds of her mantilla. For once she looked in his face and saw it without a smile, stern, menacing and purpose ful. Then he suddenly raised his hand and his smile came back like a gleam of sunshine. The hoarse sig nal of an incoming steamer's siren sounded in the har bour. Dicky called to the sentry who was pacing be fore the door : " What steamer comes ? "

"TheCoterina."

"Of the Vesuvius line?"

"Without doubt, of that line."

" Go you, picarilla," said Dicky joyously to Pasa, " to the American consul. Tell him I wish to speak with him. See that he comes at once, And look you! let

me see a different look in those eyes, for I promise

your head shall rest upon this arm to-night. "

It was an hour before the consul came. He held his green umbrella under his arm, and mopped his forehead impatiently.

" Now, see here, Maloney," he began, captiously, "you fellows seem to think you can cut up any kind of row, and expect me to pull you out of it. I'm neither the War Department nor a gold mine. This country has its laws, you know, and there's one against pounding the senses out of the regular army. You Irish are forever getting into trouble. I don't see what I can do. Anything like tobacco, now, to make you comfortable — or newspapers — "

"Son of Eli," interrupted Dicky, gravely, "you haven't changed an iota. That is almost a duplicate of the speech you made when old Koen's donkeys and geese got into the chapel loft, and the culprits wanted to hide in your room."

"Oh, heavens!" exclaimed the consul, hurriedly adjusting his spectacles. " Are you a Yale man, too ? Were you in that crowd ? I don't seem to remember any one with red — any one named Maloney. Such a

lot of college men seem to have misused their advan tages. One of the best mathematicians of the class of '91 is selling lottery tickets in Belize. A Cornell man dropped off here last month. He was second steward on a guano boat. I'll write to the department if you like, Maloney, Or if there's any tobacco, or news-pa-"

"There's nothing," interrupted Dicky, shortly, " but this. You go tell the captain of the Catarina that Dicky Maloney wants to see him as soon as he can conveniently come. Tell him where I am-Hurry. That's all."

The consul, glad to be let off so easily, hurried away. The captain of the Catarina, a stout man, Sicilian born, soon appeared, shoving, with little cere mony, through the guards to the jail door. The Vesuvius Fruit Company had a habit of doing things that way in Anchuria.

"I am exceeding sorry—exceeding sorry," said the captain, "to see this occur. I place myself at your service, Mr. Maloney. Whatever you need shall be furnished. Whatever you say shall be done."

Dicky looked at him unsmilingly. His red hair

could not detract from his attitude of severe dignity as he stood, tall and calm, with his now grim mouth forming a horizontal line.

" Captain De Lucco, I believe I still have funds in the hands of your company — ample and personal funds. I ordered a remittance last week. The money has not arrived. You know what is needed in this game. Money and money and more money. Why has it not been sent ? "

" By the Cristobal, " replied De Lucco, gesticulat ing, "it was despatched. Where is the Cristobal? Off Cape Antonio I spoke her with a broken shaft. A tramp coaster was towing her back to New Orleans. I brought money ashore thinking your need for it might not withstand delay. In this envelope is one thousand dollars. There is more if you need it, Mr. Maloney."

" For the present it will suffice," said Dicky, soft ening as he crinkled the envelope and looked down at the half-inch thickness of smooth, dingy bills.

" The long green!" he said, gently, with a new rev erence in his gaze. " Is there anything it will not buy Captain?"

" I had three friends," replied De Lucco, who was a bit of a philosopher, "who had money. One of them speculated in stocks and made ten million; an other is in heaven, and the third married a poor girl whom he loved."

"The answer, then," said Dicky, "is held by the Almighty, Wall Street and Cupid. So, the question remains."

"This," queried the captain, including Dicky's surroundings in a significant gesture of his hand, " is it — it is not — it is not connected with the business of your little shop ? There is no failure in your plans ? "

" No, no," said Dicky. " This is merely the result of a little private affair of mine, a digression from the regular line of business. They say for a complete life a man must know poverty, love and war. But they don't go well together, capitan mio. No; there is no failure in my business. The little shop is doing very well."

When the captain had departed Dicky called the sergeant of the jail squad and asked:

" Am I preso by the military or by the civil author ity?"

"Surely there is no martial law in effect now, senor,"

" Bueno. Now go or send to the alcalde, the Jucz de la Paz and the Jefe de los Policios. Tell them I am prepared at once to satisfy the demands of justice. A folded bill of the " long green " slid into the ser geant's hand.

Then Dicky's smile came back again, for he knew that the hours of his captivity were numbered; and he hummed, in time with the sentry's tread:

" They're hanging men and women now, For lacking of the green."

So, that night Dicky sat by the window of the room oyer his shop and his little saint sat close by, working at something silken and dainty. Dicky was thought ful and grave. His red hair was in an unusual state of disorder. Pasa's fingers often ached to smooth and arrange it, but Dicky would never allow it. He was poring, to-night, over a great litter of maps and books and papers on his table until that per pendicular line came between his brows that always distressed Pasa. Presently she went and brought

his hat, and stood with it until he looked up, in quiringly.

" It is sad for you here," she explained. " Go out and drink vino bianco. Come back when you get that smile you used to wear. That is what I wish to see."

Dicky laughed and threw down his papers. " The vino bianco stage is past. It has served its turn. Perhaps, after all, there was less entered my mouth and more my ears than people thought. But, there will be no more maps or frowns to-night. I promise you that. Come."

They sat upon a reed silleta at the window and watched the quivering gleams from the lights of the Catarina reflected in the harbour.

Presently Pasa rippled out one of her infrequent chirrups of audible laughter.

" I was thinking," she began, anticipating Dicky's question, "of the foolish things girls Lave in their minds. Because I went to school in the States I used to have ambitions. Nothing less than to be he pres ident's wife would satisfy me. And, look, thou red picaroon, to what obscure fate thou hast stolen me!"

" Don't give up hope," said Dicky, smiling. More than one Irishman has been the ruler of a South American country. There was a dictator of Chili named O'Higgins. Why not a President Maloney, of Anchuria ? Say the word, santita mia, and we'll make the race."

"No, no, no, thou red-haired, reckless one!" sighed Pasa; "I am content" — she laid her head against his arm — " here."

CHAPTER SIXTEEN

Rouge et Noir

IT has been indicated that disaffection followed the elevation of Losada to the presidency. This feeling continued to grow. Throughout the en tire republic there seemed to be a spirit of silent, sullen discontent. Even the old Liberal party to which Goodwin, Zavalla and other patriots had lent their aid was disappointed. Losada had failed to become a popular idol. Fresh taxes, fresh import duties and, more than all, his tolerance of the out rageous oppression of citizens by the military had rendered him the most obnoxious president since the despicable Alforan. The majority of his own cabi net were out of sympathy with him. The army, which he had courted by giving it license to

tyrannize, had been his main, and thus far adequate

support.

But the most impolitic of the administration's moves had been when it antagonized the Vesuvius Fruit Company, an organization plying twelve steam ers and with a cash capital somewhat larger than Anchuria's surplus and debt combined.

Reasonably, an established concern like the Vesu vius would become irritated at having a small, retail republic with no rating at all attempt to squeeze it. So, when the government proxies applied for a sub sidy they encountered a polite refusal. The presi dent at once retaliated by clapping an export duty of one real per bunch on bananas — a thing unprece dented in fruit-growing countries. The Vesuvius Company had invested large sums in wharves and plantations along the Anchurian coast, their agents had erected fine homes in the towns where they had their headquarters, and heretofore had worked with the republic in good-will and with advantage to both. It would lose an immense sum if compelled to move out. The selling price of bananas from Vera Cruz to Trinidad was three reals per bunch. This new

duty of one real would have ruined the fruit growers in Anchuria and have seriously discommoded the Vesuvius Company had it declined to pay it. But for some reason, the Vesuvius continued to buy An-churian fruit, paying four reals for it; and not suffer ing the growers to bear the loss.

This apparent victory deceived His Excellency; and he began to hunger for more of it. He sent an emissary to request a conference with a representa tive of the fruit company. The Vesuvius sent Mr. Franzoni, a little, stout, cheerful man, always cool, and whistling airs from Verdi's operas. Seiior Espi-rition, of the office of the Minister of Finance, at tempted the sandbagging in behalf of Anchuria. The meeting took place in the cabin of the Salvador, of the Vesuvius line.

Senor Espirition opened negotiations by announc ing that the government contemplated the building of a railroad to skirt the alluvial coast lands. After touching upon the benefits such a road would confer upon the interests of the Vesuvius, he reached the definite suggestion that a contribution to the road's expenses of, say, fifty thousand pesos

would not be more than an equivalent to benefits received.

Mr. Franzoni denied that his company would re ceive any benefits from a contemplated road. As its representative he must decline to contribute fifty thousand pesos. But he would assume the respon sibility of offering twenty-five.

Did Senor Espirition understand Senor Franzoni to mean twenty-five thousand pesos ?

By no means. Twenty-five pesos. And in silver; not in gold.

"Your offer insults my government," cried Sefior Espirition, rising, with indignation.

"Then," said Mr. Franzoni, in a warning tone, "we will change it."

The offer was never changed. Could Mr. Fran zoni have meant the government ?

This was the state of affairs in Anchuria when the winter season opened at Coralio at the end of the second year of Losada's administration. So, when the government and society made its annual exodu? to the seashore it was evident that the presidential advent would not be celebrated by unlimited rejoic

ing. The tenth of November was the day set for the entrance into Coralio of the gay company from the capital. A narrow-guage railroad runs twenty miles into the interior from Solitas. The government party travels by carriage from San Mateo to this road's terminal point, and proceeds by train to Soli tas. From here they march in grand procession to Coralio where, on the day of their coming, festivities and ceremonies abound. But this season saw an ominous dawning of the tenth of November.

Although the rainy season was over, the day seemed to hark back to reeking June. A fine drizzle of rain fell all during the forenoon. The procession entered Coralio amid a strange silence.

President Losada was an elderly man, grizzly bearded, with a considerable ratio of Indian blood revealed in his cinnamon complexion. His carriage headed the procession, surrounded and guarded by Captain Cruz and his famous troop of one hundred light horse "El Ciento Huilando" Colonel Rocas followed, with a regiment of the regular army.

The president's sharp, beady eyes glanced about him for the expected demonstration of welcome; but

he faced a stolid, indifferent array of citizens. Sight seers the Anchurians are by birth and habit, and they turned out to their last able-bodied unit to witness the scene; but they maintained an accusive silence. They crowded the streets to the very wheel ruts; they covered the red tile roofs to the eaves, but there was never a "viva" from them. No wreathes of palm and lemon branches or gorgeous strings of paper roses hung from the windows and balconies as was the custom. There was an apathy, a dull, dissent ing disapprobation, that was the more ominous be cause it puzzled. No one feared an outburst, a revolt of the discontents, for they had no leader. The president and those loyal to him had never even heard whispered a name among them cap able of crystallizing the dissatisfaction into op position. No, there could be no danger. The people always procured a new idol before they destroyed an old one.

At length, after a prodigious galloping and cur vetting of red-sashed majors, gold-laced colonels and epauletted generals, the procession formed for its annual progress down the Calle Grande to the Casa

Morena, where the ceremony of welcome to the visiting president always took place.

The Swiss band led the line of march. After it pranced the local comandante, mounted, and a de tachment of his treops. Next came a carriage with four members of the cabinet, conspicuous among them the Minister of War, old General Pilar, with his white moustache and his soldierly bearing. Then the president's vehicle, containing also the Ministers of Finance and State; and surrounded by Captain Cruz's light horse formed in a close double file of fours. Following them, the rest of the officials of state, the judges and distinguished military and social ornaments of public and private life.

As the band struck up, and the movement began, like a bird of ill-omen the Valhalla, the swiftest steam ship of the Vesuvius line, glided into the harbour in plain view of the president and his train. Of course, there was nothing menacing about its arrival — a business firm does not go to war with a nation — but it reminded Senor Espirition and others in those carriages that the Vesuvius Fruit Company was un doubtedly carrying something up its sleeve for them.

By the time the van of the procession had reached the government building, Captain Cronin, of the Valhalla, and Mr. Vincenti, member of the Vesuvius Company, had landed and were pushing their way, bluff, hearty and nonchalant, through the crowd on the narrow sidewalk. Clad in white linen, big, debonair, with an air of good-humoured authority, they made conspicuous figures among the dark mass of unimposing Anchurians, as they penetrated to within a few yards of the steps of the Casa Morena. Looking easily above the heads of the crowd, they perceived another that towered above the under sized natives. It was the fiery poll of Dicky Maloney against the wall close by the lower step; and his broad, seductive grin showed that he recognized their presence.

Dicky had attired himself becomingly for the fes tive occasion in a well-fitting black suit. Pasa was close by his side, her head covered with the ubiquit ous black mantilla.

Mr. Vincenti looked at her attentively.

"Botticelli's Madonna," he remarked, gravely. "I wonder when she got into the game. I don't like

his getting tangled with the women. I hoped he would keep away from them."

Captain Cronin's laugh almost drew attention from the parade.

"With that head of hair! Keep away from the women! And a Maloney! Hasn't he got a licence ? But, nonsense aside, what do you think of the pros pects ? It's a species of filibustering out of my line."

Vincenti glanced again at Dicky's head and smiled.

"Rouge et noir" he said. "There you have it. Make your play, gentlemen. Our money is on the red."

" The lad's game," said Cronin, with a commend ing look at the tall, easy figure by the steps. " But 'tis all like fly-by-night theatricals to me. The talk's bigger than the stage; there's a smell of gasoline in the air, and they're their own audience and scene-shifters."

They ceased talking, for General Pilar had de scended from the first carriage and had taken his stand upon the top step of Casa Morena. As the oldest member of the cabinet, custom had decreed that he should make the address of welcome, presenting the keys of the official residence to the president
at its close.

General Pilar was one of the most distinguished citizens of the republic. Hero of three wars and in numerable revolutions, he was an honoured guest at European courts and camps. An eloquent speaker and a friend to the people, he represented the highest type of the Anchurians.

Holding in his hand the gilt keys of Casa Morena, he began his address in a historical form, touching upon each administration and the advance of civili zation and prosperity from the first dim striving after liberty down to present times. Arriving at the regime of President Losada, at which point, accord ing to precedent, he should have delivered a eulogy upon its wise conduct and the happiness of the peo ple, General Pilar paused. Then he silently held up the bunch of keys high above his head, with his eyes closely regarding it. The ribbon with which they were bound fluttered in the breeze.

"It still blows," cried the speaker, exultantly. " Citizens of Anchuria, give thanks to the saints this night that our air is still free."

Thus disposing of Losada's administration, he abruptly reverted to that of Olivarra, Anchuria's most popular ruler. Olivarra had been assassinated nine years before while in the prime of life and useful ness. A faction of the Liberal party led by Losada himself had been accused of the deed. Whether guilty or not, it was eight years before the ambitious and scheming Losada had gained his goal.

Upon this theme General Pilar's eloquence was loosed. He drew the picture of the beneficent Oli varra with a loving hand. He reminded the people of the peace, the security and the happiness they had enjoyed during that period. He recalled in vivid detail and with significant contrast the last winter sojourn of President Olivarra in Coralio, when his appearance at their fiestas was the signal for thundering vivas of love and approbation.

The first public expression of sentiment from the people that day followed. A low, sustained murmur went among them like the surf rolling along the shore.

"Ten dollars to a dinner at the Saint Charles," remarked Mr. Vincenti, " that rouge wins."

"I never bet against my own interests," said Captain Cronin, lighting a cigar. "Long-winded old boy, for his age. What's he talking about ? "

"My Spanish," replied Vincenti, "runs about ten words to the minute; his is something around two hundred. Whatever he's saying, he's getting them warmed up."

" Friends and brothers," General Pilar was saying, "could I reach out my hand this day across the lamentable silence of the grave to Olivarra 'the Good,' to the ruler who was one of you, whose tears fell when you sorrowed, and whose smile followed your joy — I would bring him back to you, but — Olivarra is dead — dead at the hands of a craven assassin!"

The speaker turned and gazed boldly into the car riage of the president. His arm remained extended aloft as if to sustain his peroration. The president was listening, aghast, at this remarkable address of welcome. He was sunk back upon his seat, trem bling with rage and dumb surprise, his dark hands tightly gripping the carriage cushions.

Half rising, he extended one arm toward the

speaker, and shouted a harsh command at Captain Cruz. The leader of the " Flying Hundred " sat his horse, immovable, with folded arms, giving no sign of having heard. Losada sank back again, his dark features distinctly paling.

" Who says that Olivarra is dead ? " suddenly cried the speaker, his voice, old as he was, sounding like a battle trumpet. " His body lies in the grave, but to the people he loved he has bequeathed his spirit

— yes, more — his learning, his courage, his kindness

— yes, more — his youth, his image — people of Anchuria, have you forgotten Ramon, the son of Olivarra?"

Cronin and Vincenti, watching closely, saw Dicky Maloney suddenly raise his hat, tear off his shock of red hair, leap up the steps and stand at the side of General Pilar. The Minister of War laid his arm across the young man's shoulders. All who had known President Olivarra saw again his same lion-like pose, the same frank, undaunted expression, the same high forehead with the peculiar line of the clustering, crisp black hair.

General Pilar was an experienced orator. He

seized the moment of breathless silence that pre ceded the storm.

"Citizens of Anchuria," he trumpeted, holding aloft the keys to Casa Morena, " I am here to deliver these keys — the keys to your homes and liberty -to your chosen president. Shall I deliver them to Enrico Olivarra's assassin, or to his son ? "

"Olivarra! Olivarra!" the crowd shrieked and howled. All vociferated the magic name — men, women, children and the parrots.

And the enthusiasm was not confined to the blood of the plebs. Colonel Rocas ascended the steps and laid his sword theatrically at young Ramon Olivarra's feet. Four members of the cabinet embraced him. Captain Cruz gave a command, and twenty of El Ciento Huilando dismounted and arranged them selves in a cordon about the steps of Casa Morena.

But Ramon Olivarra seized that moment to prove himself a born genius and politician. He waved those soldiers aside, and descended the steps to the street. There, without losing his dignity or the dis tinguished elegance that the loss of his red hair brought him, he took the proletariat to his bosom —

the barefooted, the dirty, Indians, Caribs, babies, beggars, old, young, saints, soldiers and sinners—• he missed none of them.

While this act of the drama was being presented, the scene shifters had been busy at the duties that had been assigned to them. Two of Cruz's dragoons had seized the bridle reins of Losada's horses; others formed a close guard around the carnage; and they galloped off with the tyrant and his two unpopular Ministers. No doubt a place had been prepared for them. There are a number of well-barred stone apartments in Coralio.

"Rouge wins," said Mr. Vincenti, calmly light ing another cigar.

Captain Cronin had been intently watching the vicinity of the stone steps for some time.

" Good boy!" he exclaimed suddenly, as if relieved. " I wondered if he was going to forget his Kathleen Mavourneen."

Young Olivarra had reascended the steps and spoken a few words to General Pilar. Then that distinguished veteran descended to the ground and approached Pasa, who still stood, wonder-eyed.

Cabbages and Kings 1 where Dicky had left her. With his plumed hat in his hand, and his medals and decorations shining on his breast, the general spoke to her and gave her his arm, and they went up the stone steps of the Casa Morena together. And then Ramon Olivarra stepped forward and took both her hands before all the people.

And while the cheering was breaking out afresh everywhere, Captain Cronin and Mr. Vincenti turned and walked back toward the shore where the gig was waiting for them.

"There'll be another 'presidente proclamada' in the morning." said Mr. Vincenti, musingly. " As a rule they are not as reliable as the elected ones, but this youngster seems to have some good stuff in him. He planned and manoeuvred the entire campaign. Olivarra's widow, you know, was wealthy. After her husband was assassinated she went to the States, and educated her son at Yale. The Vesuvius Company hunted him up, and backed him in the little game."

" It's a glorious thing," said Cronin, half jestingly, " to be able to discharge a government, and insert one of your own choosing, in these days."

" Oh, it is only a matter of business," said Vincenti, stopping and offering the stump of his cigar to a mon key that swung down from a lime tree; " and that is what moves the world of to-day. That extra real on the price of bananas had to go. We took the short est way of removing it."

CHAPTER SEVENTEEN Two Recalls

1 HERE remains three duties to be performed be fore the curtain falls upon the patched comedy. Two have been promised: the third is no less obligatory.

It was set forth in the programme of this tropic vaudeville that it would be made known why Shorty O'Day, of the Columbia Detective Agency, lost his position. Also that Smith should come again to tell us what mystery he followed that night on the shores of Anchuria when he strewed so many cigar stumps around the cocoanut palm during his lonely night vigil on the beach. These things were promised; but a bigger thing yet remains to be accomplished — the clearing up of a seeming wrong that has been done according to the array of chronicled facts (truthfully

set forth) that have been presented. And one voice, speaking, shall do these three things.

Two men sat on a stringer of a North River pier in the City of New York. A steamer from the tropics had begun to unload bananas and oranges on the pier. Now and then a banana or two would fall from an overripe bunch, and one of the two men would sham ble forward, seize the fruit and return to share it with his companion.

One of the men was in the ultimate stage of deteri oration. As far as rain and wind and sun could wreck the garments he wore, it had been done. In his person the ravages of drink were as plainly visible. And yet, upon his high-bridged, rubicund nose was jauntily perched a pair of shining and flawless gold-rimmed glasses.

The other man was not so far gone upon the de scending Highway of the Incompetents. Truly, the flower of his manhood had gone to seed — seed that, perhaps, no soil might sprout. But there were still cross-cuts along where he travelled through which he might yet regain the pathway of usefulness without disturbing the slumbering Miracles. This man was

short and compactly built. He had an oblique, dead eye, like that of a sting-ray, and the moustache of a cocktail mixer. We know the eye and the moustache; we know that Smith of the luxurious yacht, the gor geous raiment, the mysterious mission, the magic dis appearance, has come again, though shorn of the ac cessories of his former state.

At his third banana, the man with the nose glasses spat it from him with a shudder.

" Deuce take all fruit!" he remarked, in a patrician tone of disgust. " I lived for two years where these things grow. The memory of their taste lingers with you. The oranges are not so bad.

Just see if you can gather a couple of them, O'Day, when the next broken crate comes up. "

" Did you live down with the monkeys ? " asked the other, made tepidly garrulous by the sunshine and the alleviating meal of juicy fruit. "I was down there, once myself. But only for a few hours. That was when I was with the Columbia Detective Agency. The monkey people did me up. I'd have my job yet if it hadn't been for them. I'll tell you about it.

** One day the chief sent a note around to the office that read: * Send O'Day here at once for a big piece of business.' I was the crack detective of the agency at that time. They always handed me the big jobs. The address the chief wrote from was down in the Wall Street district.

" When I got there I found him in a private office with a lot of directors who were looking pretty fuzzy. They stated the case. The president of the Republic Insurance Company had skipped with about a tenth of a million dollars in cash. The directors wanted him back pretty bad, but they wanted the money worse. They said they needed it. They had traced the old gent's movements to where he boarded a tramp fruit steamer bound for South America that same morning with his daughter and a big gripsack — all the family he had.

" One of the directors had his steam yacht coaled and with steam up, ready for a trip; and he turned her over to me, cart blongsh. In four hours I was on board of her, and hot on the trail of the fruit tub. I had a pretty good idea where old Wahrfield — that was his name, J. Churchill Wahrfield — would head for.

At that time we had a treaty with about every foreign country except Belgium and that banana republic, Anchuria. There wasn't a photo of old Wahrfield to be had in New York — he had been foxy there — but I had his description. And besides, the lady with him would be a dead-give-away anywhere. She was one of the high-flyers in Society — not the kind that have their pictures in the Sunday papers — but the real sort that open chrysanthemum shows and chris ten battleships.

" Well, sir, we never got a sight of that fruit tub on the road. The ocean is a pretty big place; and I guess we took different paths across it. But we kept going toward this Anchuria, where the fruiter was bound for.

" We struck the monkey coast one afternoon about four. There was a ratty-looking steamer off shore taking on bananas. The monkeys were loading her up with big barges. It might be the one the old man had taken, and it might not. I went ashore to look around. The scenery was pretty good. I never saw any finer on the New York stage. I struck an Ameri can on shore, a big, cool chap, standing around with

the monkeys. He showed me the consul's office. The consul was a nice young fellow. He said the fruiter was the Karlscfin, running generally to New Orleans, but took her last cargo to New York. Then I was sure my people were on board, although everybody told me that no passengers had landed. I didn't think they would land until after dark, for they might have been shy about it on account of seeing that yacht of mine hanging around. So, all I had to do was to wait and nab 'em when they came ashore. I couldn't arrest old Wahrfield without extradition pa pers, but my play was to get the cash. They gener ally give up if you strike 'em when they're tired and rattled and short on nerve.

"After dark I sat under a cocoanut tree on the beach for a while, and then I walked around and in vestigated that town some, and it was enough to give you the lions. If a man could stay in New York and be honest, he'd better do it than to hit that monkey town with a million.

"Dinky little mud houses; grass over your shoe tops in the streets; ladies in low-neck-and-short-sleeves walking around smoking cigars; tree frogs

rattling like a hose cart going to a ten blow; big mountains dropping gravel in the back yards, and the sea licking the paint off in front — no, sir — a man had better be in God's country living on free lunch than there.

" The main street ran along the beach, and I walked down it, and then turned up a kind of lane where the houses were made of poles and straw. I wanted to see what the monkeys did when they weren't climbing cocoanut trees. The very first shack I looked in I saw my people. They must have come ashore while I was promenading. A man about fifty, smooth face, heavy eyebrows, dressed in black broadcloth, looking like he was just about to say, * Can any little boy in the Sunday school answer that?' He was freezing on to a grip that weighed like a dozen gold bricks, and a swell girl — a regular peach, with a Fifth Ave nue cut—was sitting on a wooden chair. An old black woman was fixing some coffee and beans on a table. The light they had come from a lantern hung on a nail. I went and stood in the door, and they looked at me, and I said:

"'Mr. Wahrfield, you are my prisoner. I hope,
for the lady's sake, you will take the matter sensibly. You know why I want you.'

" * Who are you ?' says the old gent.

"'O'Day,' says I, 'of the Columbia Detective Agency. And now, sir, let me give you a piece of good advice. You go back and take your medicine like a man. Hand 'em back the boodle; and maybe they'll let you off light. Go back easy, and I'll put in a word for you. I'll give you five minutes to decide.' I pulled out my watch and waited.

" Then the young lady chipped in. She was one of the genuine high-steppers. You could tell by the way her clothes fit and the style she had that Fifth Avenue was made for her.

"'Come inside, 5 she says. 'Don't stand in the door and disturb the whole street with that suit of clothes. Now, what is it you want ?'

' Three minutes gone,' I said. ' I'll tell you again while the other two tick off.

' You'll admit being the president of the Repub lic, won't you ?'

"' I am,' says he.

"'Well, then,' says I, 'it ought to be plain to you.
Wanted, in New York, J. Churchill Wahrfield, presi dent of the Republic Insurance Company.

"'Also the funds belonging to said company, no\v in that grip, in the unlawful possession of said J. Churchill Wahrfield.'

"' Oh-h-h-h!' says the young lady, as if she was thinking,' you want to take us back to New York ?'

"'To take Mr. Wahrfield. There's no charge against you, miss. There'll be no objection, of course, to your returning with your father.'

"Of a sudden the girl gave a tiny scream and grabbed the old boy around the neck. ' Oh, father, father! 5 she says, kind of contralto, 'can this be true? Have you taken money that is not yours? Speak, father!' It made you shiver to hear the tremolo stop she put on her voice.

"The old boy looked pretty bughouse when she first grappled him, but she went on, whispering in his ear and patting his off shoulder till he stood still, but sweating a little.

" She got him to one side and they talked together a minute, and then he put on some gold eyeglasses and walked up and handed me the grip.

V

"'Mr. Detective,' he says, talking a little broken, ' I conclude to return with you. I have finished to discover that life on this desolate and displeased coast would be worse than to die, itself. I will go back and hurl myself upon the mercy of the Republic Com pany. Have you brought a sheep ?'

" ' Sheep! ' says I; ' I haven't a single —'

" * Ship, 5 cut in the young lady. ' Don't get funny. Father is of German birth, and doesn't speak perfect English. How did you come ?'

" The girl was all broke up. She had a handker chief to her face, and kept saying every little bit,' Oh, father, father!' She walked up to me and laid her lily-white hand on the clothes that had pained her at first. I smelt a million violets. She was a lulu. I told her I came in a private yacht.

' * Mr. O'Day,' she says. ' Oh, take us away from this horrid country at once. Can you! Will you! Say you will.'

" * I'll try,' I said, concealing the fact that I was dy ing to get them en salt water before they could change their mind.

"One thing they both kicked against was going through the town to the boat landing. Said they dreaded publicity, and now that they were going to re turn, they had a hope that the thing might yet be kept out of the papers. They swore they wouldn't go un less I got them out to the yacht without any one know ing it, so I agreed to humour them.

"The sailors who rowed me ashore were playing billiards in a bar-room near the water, waiting for or ders, and I proposed to have them take the boat down the beach half a mile or so, and take us up there. How to get them word was the question, for I couldn't leave the grip with the prisoner, and I couldn't take it with me, not knowing but what the monkeys might stick me up.

"The young lady says the old coloured woman would take them a note. I sat down and wrote it, and gave it to the dame with plain directions what to do, and she grins like a baboon and shakes her head.

" Then Mr. Wahrfield handed her a string of for eign dialect, and she nods her head and says, 'See, senor,' maybe fifty times, and lights out with the note.

" ' Old Augusta only understands German,' said Miss Wahrfield, smiling at me. ' We stopped in her house to ask where we could find lodging, and she in sisted upon our having coffee. She tells us she was raised in a German family in San Domingo.'

" * Very likely/ I said. ' But you can search me for German words, except nix verstay and nock einst. I would have called that" See, senor " French, though, on a gamble/

" Well, we three made a sneak around the edge of town so as not to be seen. We got tangled in vines and ferns and the banana bushes and tropical scenery a good deal. The monkey suburbs was as wild as places in Central Park. We came out on the beach a good half mile below. A brown chap was lying asleep under a cocoanut tree, with a ten-foot musket beside him. Mr. Wahrfield takes up the gun and pitches it into the sea. 'The coast is guarded/ he says. 'Rebellion and plots ripen like fruit.' He pointed to the sleeping man, who never stirred. * Thus/ he says, ' they perform trusts. Children!'

" I saw our boat coming, and I struck a match and lit a piece of newspaper to show them where we were. In thirty minutes we were on board the yacht.

"The first thing, Mr. Wahrfield and his daughter and I took the grip into the owner's cabin, opened it up, and took an inventory. There was one hundred and five thousand dollars, United States treasury notes in it, besides a lot of diamond jewelry and a couple of hundred Havana cigars. I gave the old man the cigars and a receipt for the rest of the lot, as agent for the company, and locked the stuff up in my private quarters.

" I never had a pleasanter trip than that one. After we got to sea the young lady turned out to be the jolli-est ever. The very first time we sat down to dinner, and the steward filled her glass with champagne — that director's yacht was a regular floating Waldorf-Astoria — she winks at me and-says, ' What's the use to borrow trouble, Mr. Fly Cop ? Here's hoping you may live to eat the hen that scratches on your grave.* There was a piano on board, and she sat down to it and sung better than you give up two cases to hear plenty times. She knew about nine operas clear through. She was sure enough bon ton and swell. She wasn't one of the 'among others present* kind; she belonged on the special mention list!

"The old man, too, perked up amazingly on the

way. He passed the cigars, and says to me once, quite chipper, out of a cloud of smoke, ' Mr. O'Day, somehow I think the Republic Company will not give me the much trouble. Guard well the gripvalise of the money, Mr. O'Day, for that it must be returned to them that it belongs when we finish to arrive.'

" When we landed in New York I 'phoned to the chief to meet us in that director's office. We got in a cab and went there. I carried the grip, and we walked in, and I was pleased to see that the chief had got together that same old crowd of moneybugs with pink faces and white vests to see us march in. I set the grip on the table. ' There's the money,' I said.

"' And your prisoner ?' said the chief.

"I pointed to Mr. Wahrfield, and he stepped for ward and says:

* The honour of a word with you, sir, to explain.'

"He and the chief went into another room and stayed ten minutes ? When they came back the chief looked as black as a ton of coal.

"' Did this gentleman,' he says to me, ' have this valise in his possession when you first saw him ?'

"'He did,' said I.

"The chief took up the grip and handed it to the prisoner with a bow, and says to the director crowd-' Do any of you recognize this gentleman ? *

" They all shook their pink faces.

"' Allow me to present,' he goes on,' Sefior Mira-flores, president of the republic of Anchuria. The senor has generously consented to overlook this out rageous blunder, on condition that we undertake to secure him against the annoyance of public comment. It is a concession on his part to overlook an insult for which he might claim international redress. I think we can gratefully promise him secrecy in the matter.'

" They gave him a pink nod all round.

: "O'Day,' he says to me. * As a private detective you're wasted. In a war, where kidnapping govern ments is in the rules, you'd be invaluable. Come down to the office at eleven.'

" I knew what that meant.

"' So that's the president of the monkeys,' says I, ' Well, why couldn't he have said so ?'

"Wouldn't it jar you?"

CHAPTER EIGHTEEN

The Vitagraphoscope

VAUDEVILLE is intrinsically episodic and dis continuous. Its audiences do not demand de nouements. Sufficient unto each "turn" is the evil thereof. No one cares how many romances the singing comedienne may have had if she can capably sustain the limelight and a high note or two. The audiences reck not if the performing dogs get to the pound the moment they have jumped through their last hoop. They do not desire bulletins about the possible injuries received by the comic bicyclist who retires head-first from the stage in a crash of (property) china-ware. Neither do they consider that their seat coupons entitle them to be instructed whether or no there is a

sentiment between the lady solo banjoist and the

Irish monologist.

Therefore let us have no lifting of the curtain upon a tableau of the united lovers, backgrounded by de feated villainy and derogated by the comic, osculating maid and butler, thrown in as a sop to the Cerberi of the fifty-cent seats.

But our programme ends with a brief "turn" or two; and then to the exits. Whoever sits the show out may find, if he will, the slender thread that binds together, though ever so slightly, the story that, per haps, only the Walrus will understand.

Extracts from a letter from the first vice-president of the Republic Insurance Company, of New York City, to Frank Goodwin, of Coralio, Republic of Anchuria.

My Dear Mr. Goodwin: —Your communication per Messrs. Rowland and Fourchet, of New Orleans, has reached us. Also their draft on N. Y. for $100,-000, the amount abstracted from the funds of this company by the late J. Churchill Wahrfield, its for mer president. . . . The officers and directors unite in requesting me to express to you their sincere esteem and thanks for your prompt and much appre-

ciated return of the entire missing sum within two weeks from the time of its disappearance. . . . Can assure you that the matter will not be allowed to receive the least publicity. . . . Regret exceed ingly the distressing death of Mr. Wahrfield by his own hand, but . . . . Congratulations on your marriage to Miss Wahrfield . . . many charms, winning manners, noble and womanly nature and en vied position in the best metropolitan society. . . . Cordially yours,

Lucius E. APPLEGATE, First Vice-President the Republic Insurance Company.

The Vitagraphoscope

(Moving Pictures) The Last Sausage

SCENE — An Artist's Studio. The artist, a young man of prepossessing appearance, sits in a dejected attitude, amid a litter of sketches, with his head resting upon his hand. An oil stove stands on a pine box in the centre of the studio. The artist rises, tightens his waist belt to another hole, and lights the stove. He goes to a tin bread box, half-hidden by

a screen, takes out a solitary link of sausage, turns the box upside-down to show that there is no more, and chucks the sausage into a frying-pan, which he sets upon the stove. The flame of the stove goes out, showing that there is no more oil. The artist, in evident despair, seizes the sausage, in a sudden access of rage, and hurls it violently from him. At the same time a door opens, and a man who enters receives the sausage forcibly against his nose. He seems to cry out; and is observed to make a dance step or two, vigorously. The newcomer is a ruddy-faced, active, keen-looking man, apparently of Irish ancestry. Next he is observed to laugh immoderately; he kicks over the stove; he claps the artist (who is vainly striving to grasp his hand) vehemently upon the back. Then he goes through a pantomime which to the sufficiently intelligent spectator reveals that he has acquired large sums of money by trading pot-metal hatchets and razors to the Indians of the Cordillera Mountains for gold dust. He draws a roll of money as large as a small loaf of bread from his pocket, and waves it above his head, while at the same time he makes pantomime of drinking from a glass. The

artist hurriedly secures his hat, and the two leave the studio together.

The Writing on the Sands

SCENE — The Beach at Nice. A woman, beau tiful, still young, exquisitely clothed, complacent, poised, reclines near the water, idly scrawling letters in the sand with the staff of her silken parasol. The beauty of her face is audacious; her languid pose is one that you feel to be impermanent — you wait, ex pectant, for her to spring or glide or crawl, like a panther that has unaccountably become stock-still. She idly scrawls in the sand; and the word that she always writes is " Isabel." A man sits a few yards away. You can see that they are companions, even if no longer comrades. His face is dark and smooth, and almost inscrutable — but not quite. The two speak little together. The man also scratches on the sand with his cane. And the word that he writes is "Anchuria." And then he looks out where the Mediterranean and the sky intermingle, with death in his gaze.

The Wilderness and Thou SCENE — The Borders of a Gentleman's Estate in a Tropical Land. An old Indian, with a mahogany -coloured face, is trimming the grass on a grave by a mangrove swamp. Presently he rises to his feet and walks slowly toward a grove that is shaded by the gathering, brief twilight. In the edge of the grove stand a man who is stalwart, with a kind and courte ous air, and a woman of a serene and clear-cut loveli ness. When the old Indian comes up to them the man drops money in his hand. The grave-tender, with the stolid pride of his race, takes it as his due, and goes his way. The two in the edge of the grove turn back along the dim pathway, and walk close, close — for, after all, what is the world at its best but a little round field of the moving pictures with two walking together in it ?

THE END

Made in the USA
Middletown, DE
10 September 2023